NANCY WARREN

DIAMONDS AND DAGGERS

VAMPIRE KNITTING CLUB
BOOK ELEVEN

ISBN: ebook 978-1-928145-92-9

ISBN: print 978-1-928145-91-2

Ambleside Publishing

INTRODUCTION

Missing jewels, a witch's dagger and murder...

Just a regular day at Cardinal Woolsey's Knitting and Yarn Shop in Oxford.

When glamorous vampire Sylvia discovers a movie company is remaking one of her most famous silent films, she's determined to get some creative input and decides to make knitting shop owner, Lucy, the beneficiary of her estate. Lucy will front for Sylvia in dealing with the movie executives who want to recreate the priceless Cartier jewels made especially for the original movie and still owned by Sylvia.

Meanwhile, Lucy's moving along in her witch's training. It's time to choose her own athame, a dagger that she'll use for spells.

With all that going on, she's barely got time to run a knitting shop, never mind solve another murder.

This is book II in the Vampire Knitting Club. From a USA Today bestselling author, these stories are cozy, clean, with quirky characters, a too-smart cat, and lots of magic and mayhem. Each can be read alone.

Get the origin story of Rafe, the gorgeous, sexy vampire in *The Vampire Knitting Club* series, for free when you join Nancy's no-spam newsletter at NancyWarrenAuthor.com.

Come join Nancy in her private Facebook group where we talk about books, knitting, pets and life. www.facebook.com/groups/NancyWarrenKnitwits

DIAMONDS AND DAGGERS

CHAPTER 1

"*L*ucy, I have decided to make you the beneficiary of my estate," Sylvia Strand announced with drama. Of course, having been a famous stage and screen actress in the silent era, Sylvia was always big on drama.

She had come to visit me in my Oxford flat above Cardinal Woolsey's Knitting and Yarn Shop, and she was alone, which was odd. Normally she and Agnes Bartlett, my grandmother, were inseparable. She looked at me expectantly, but I wasn't sure how to react. Sylvia was a vampire so chances were that I, a mere mortal, was going to be pushing up daisies for centuries while she was still enjoying her wealth.

I sensed there was more going on here than a desire to put her affairs in order. However, I didn't want to appear rude, so I said, "Thank you."

There was a pause. She seemed to expect more. "I'm worth a great deal, you know. My jewels alone are worth a small fortune." Her lips curved in a smile. "Perhaps not so small."

I really didn't want to play games with Sylvia. She always won. So, I said, "Unless there's something I don't know, you'll be wearing your jewels long after I'm gone."

"One never knows," she said vaguely. And then suddenly dropped the attitude and sat on one of the chintz chairs in my living room, inviting me to sit opposite her on the couch. "Oh, all right. I need your help."

Nyx came in the window, sniffed at Sylvia's ankles and jumped onto my lap. I was happy to have my familiar close while the glamorous vampire explained whatever favor she wanted.

"It's quite simple, really. A film company is remaking *The Professor's Wife*, one of my most famous films."

I knew this, and she'd been furious when she found out. Now she seemed to have changed her tune. "Okay," I said cautiously.

"The company contacted my estate's lawyer, Bertram Winthrop."

Her estate's lawyer. "Is he...?"

"Undead? Oh, yes. I never do business with daywalkers. Too temporary."

"Right."

"Bertram tells me Rune Films want to pay homage to the original. They intend to recreate the set of jewels used in the film."

"What jewels?"

She chuckled softly. "Cartier designed a unique set for me to wear in the movie, and in the terms of my contract, I was able to keep them."

"Cartier designed jewelry especially for you?"

"Of course. Jacques was a good friend. I was paid in those

2

jewels. The diamonds were flawless, the emeralds remarkable in color, and the design is pure deco."

"Wow. That was quite the paycheck."

"I've kept them always. Now, I want you to wear them."

Suddenly I felt like there wasn't enough air in the room. "You want me to wear a priceless set of diamonds and emeralds? Where?"

"Here in Oxford. First, you're to meet with the producers in London as my beneficiary, representing my estate."

"London?"

"That's right. You'll sign the contract giving the company the right to reproduce the jewels for the film and to have the real ones on display for a gala evening to announce the film. You will wear the jewels at this party. It will be held at St. Peters College where the film is being shot. It's very exciting for you."

I didn't feel the least bit excited. In fact, I felt faint. "Are the jewels insured?"

"How does one insure that which is priceless?" She let that hang in the air for a moment and then leaned forward. "Don't lose them."

THE VAMPIRE KNITTING club met that night, but Sylvia had sworn me to secrecy. The vampire knitters might be the closest she had to friends, but I could tell she didn't trust them, at least not with her priceless collection of jewels. Gran was in on the secret though. She looked delighted when she came upstairs through the trapdoor from the subterranean apartments that some of them shared below my shop. She said, "Lucy, isn't it exciting? You're going to be a film star."

I nearly choked, but Sylvia made a sound like she genuinely was choking. "A film star? She'll be wearing my jewels. A stunning collection that once did belong to a film star back when people understood what glamour really was."

I had to hide my smile as she struck a pose like Greta Garbo in an old black-and-white movie. Gran hastily covered over her blunder by saying, "That's what I meant, dear. Just wearing such a fabulous set of jewels will make Lucy feel like a star, I'm sure."

Sylvia sniffed. "I ought to be wearing them myself, but my lawyer insists it would be a dangerous thing to do."

I glanced at Gran, and both our eyes widened. I couldn't imagine a worse idea than Sylvia showing up when she had supposedly been dead for decades. That was the thing. If she'd been undead for centuries, she'd get away with it. But she didn't look that different from the silent screen star she had been. Wandering around the streets of Oxford, she could pass for anyone, but in the company of people who were remaking her most famous movie, there might be some seriously raised eyebrows, and that kind of scrutiny was what the local vampires always tried to avoid.

Fortunately, Sylvia knew that wearing the jewels herself was impossible. As though to take her mind off the disappointment, Gran pulled out a paper bag with the Cardinal Woolsey logo stamped on it and said, "I've had the most wonderful idea. I saw the new Teddy Lamont magazine with this darling sweater knit in a diamond stitch. And he's got a whole range of jewel-colored wools. I'm making it in red, in exactly your size, Lucy."

I loved it when the vampires knitted me sweaters. Even though I had a wardrobe full of them, it was always nice to have something new to wear around the shop. Naturally, since Gran knitted at supersonic speed, she already had the back done and part of one sleeve. At her pace, I'd be wearing the garment tomorrow. "My idea is to make one in every color. What do you think, dear? We could display them on the back wall of the shop."

I was very enthusiastic about the idea. "It would really draw people in. Gran, that's a fantastic idea."

Hester, the perennially whiny teenager, had pulled herself up into the back room as though she were dragging herself out of her coffin. She let out a huge sigh. "Nice for some. No one ever asks me if I might like to make something for the shop."

We all turned to stare at her. Hester was not known for helping others. Then Gran, who was the nicest vampire in the world, said, "I'd be thrilled for you to do one, my dear. Which color do you like best?"

Hester looked at the array of red and gold and green and sapphire blue and said, "Black."

What was the point?

Gran said, "It's not quite in keeping with our theme, though, is it? Do you think maybe you could try this blue color? It would look lovely with your eyes."

That caught her attention. Since we had a new vampire in town, a young Spaniard named Carlos, Hester had actually been attempting to improve her appearance and, at least when he was around, her attitude. Sadly, he wasn't here, so she'd reverted to the sulky Hester we all knew and didn't love.

She snapped, "Fine." And held out her hand impatiently.

Gran grew flustered. "Well, I don't have it here. I'll have to go to the front of the shop and get you everything you'll need." She glanced at me, looking apologetic. "Is that all right, Lucy?"

"I don't run the vampire knitting club. I only provide the venue. It doesn't matter to me if we're a little late starting."

And so Gran took Hester to the shop for wool and supplies for the intricate sweaters they were going to knit. I settled down with the much less glamorous hat I was knitting. I thought if I really worked at it, I could have this finished by next week. I didn't have many finished projects that I could be proud of. I really needed to start pulling my weight in the knitting department. I only wished I enjoyed knitting more. Sometimes I indulged myself with wishing that my grandmother had run a chocolate shop for me to inherit.

Or maybe a jewelry store.

Thinking about jewelry reminded me that later that evening, Sylvia wanted me to go downstairs with her and try on the Cartier set. I felt distinctly nervous at the idea of wearing her jewelry. I knew she didn't want me to, and if there'd been any other option, she'd have taken it. But there wasn't.

She seemed to think she was conferring a great favor on me. I felt the opposite. If anything went wrong, I didn't want a vampire as powerful as Sylvia holding a grudge.

The very idea sent a shiver down my spine. I told myself that nothing would happen and dug my knitting needle into the next stitch.

We did our show and tell when everyone was gathered. Dr. Christopher Weaver, a dapper man who ran a private blood bank, was working on one of his endless vests. Mabel was making a sweater that looked like a bath mat. It was truly the ugliest thing I'd ever seen, lime green festooned with big crocheted flowers in orange and purple. Still, she worked at it cheerfully.

Sylvia started when she saw the work in progress and then carefully averted her eyes as though she'd permanently damaged her eyeballs by looking at it.

Gran and Hester were both working on diamond sweaters, and Hester seemed marginally more cheerful now that she felt included.

Sylvia didn't work on anything. It was unlike her, which made me suspect that she was as nervous as I was. Carlos, the young-looking gorgeous Spaniard, arrived with a black backpack that contained his knitting. Hester immediately transformed from sulky to sweet. "I didn't think you were coming tonight," she said.

"I wasn't planning to, but I got in a tangle, and I need help." He sat beside her and pulled out something I could have made. It wasn't tangled. His tension was too tight. I'd had the same problem when I first began knitting. I felt very pleased with myself that I could both diagnose his problem and know that I had learned to loosen up with my knitting. Progress. Since he was the only other non-expert knitter in the club, I brightened up almost as much as Hester did when he came to our meetings.

She leaned in to help. "Oh, silly. You've been knitting so tightly that you can barely get your needles in the wool. And you've dropped a stitch. Let's get you back on track."

Rafe arrived about five minutes later. I knew he was there when Nyx, my black familiar, perked up and let out a happy meow. I have pretty good hearing, but hers is extraordinary. Especially when Rafe is around. He came in and apologized for being late. He glanced around the room, almost as though checking who was there, and then his gaze rested on me, and he gave me the smile that he never gives to anyone else. "Lucy, good evening."

"Hi," I said, and then I put my head down and got back to my knitting.

Okay, it wasn't exactly sweet nothings, but there were a dozen very nosy vampires overhearing our every word. Rafe had proposed to me, and I had no idea how to answer, which made everything awkward.

He settled down and pulled out his own knitting. I watched him for a couple of minutes, his long-fingered hands working with fine navy cashmere.

Carlos watched him, too, no doubt longing for the day his knitting would be that smooth and effortless. He asked, "Is that for Lucy?"

Rafe glanced up. "I beg your pardon?"

"That sweater you're knitting. Is it for Lucy?" Everyone stopped knitting and stared at him as though he'd made a bad joke. Rafe had never knit me a sweater. All the other vampires had, along with hats, scarves, mittens, leggings, dresses. But not Rafe. How had I never noticed this before?

"No," he said.

"He's afraid of the curse," Clara said to Mabel in a louder voice than she'd probably intended.

"Curse?" Carlos asked. "What curse?"

I'd stopped knitting now, too. How could there be curses even in knitting? Was nothing safe?

8

"It's just a silly superstition," Gran said, but she looked like she was trying not to smile.

"Not silly at all," Clara said. "My sister Bernice had it happen to her."

"Had what happen?" I asked, dying to know what all this was about. And what it had to do with Rafe.

"The curse of the love sweater, of course," Clara said.

Carlos and I shared a glance. Curse of the love sweater?

"Bernice was set to marry her beau," Clara continued. "A nice young man. He was a stoker on the railway. She decided to knit him a sweater. Lovely it was. Gray with red stripes. By the time she got to the second sleeve, he was stepping out with another girl. That's the love sweater curse." She shook her head. "She put that sweater away and never picked up knitting again. Died a spinster, she did."

"The curse is foolish nonsense," Sylvia snapped. But she seemed to be in a snappish mood.

"This curse then," Carlos asked, "does it only happen if you're already going out together?"

"No," Mabel said. "It's considered wise never to knit a sweater for someone you hope will one day be yours."

Rafe had his head down and kept knitting as though he were deaf to the conversation. Since I wasn't a vampire, I could still blush and felt my face getting warm. To hide it, I got more diligent with my own knitting than was usual for me.

At least I now knew why Rafe never knit me anything.

We knitted for a couple of hours, sharing gossip, and then the vampires began folding up their work. At this point, I usually went up to bed and they went out to socialize or roam the streets or whatever they did when most of Oxford was sleeping.

Tonight, I packed away my knitting and followed Gran and Sylvia toward the trap door that led down into the tunnel toward their home.

Rafe said, "Lucy. I imagined you'd be going up to bed."

I wasn't going to lie to him, and Sylvia must have known it. She said, before I could open my mouth, "I want Lucy's advice about something."

He raised an eyebrow and looked at her in a rather searching way, but when she didn't elaborate, he merely said, "I'll bid you all goodnight then." And he left.

We climbed down the rough stairway into the tunnels that ran underneath the city of Oxford. For as long as I'd been coming down here, I was always still slightly creeped out when I'd climbed down the stairs. I could smell the damp from the river that had once run under here. I stuck to the side where the stone path met the rough stone wall and where torches were burning to light our way. You'd miss the doorway that leads into the vampires' lair if you didn't know it was there. They'd left it deliberately old and decrepit-looking, but looks can be deceiving. That door was as high-tech and secure as any door in the world probably. Sylvia, Gran and I went in and instead of going straight through to Sylvia's rooms as I'd anticipated, we followed Sylvia's lead and sat in the living room. Most of the others were only returning to drop their work off before going out for the night.

Coming into their complex was a bit like entering Aladdin's cave of wonders. The furniture was opulent, and paintings, no doubt worth a fortune, hung from the walls.

Alfred, Christopher and Theodore were headed to a

poker game and soon left. Hester and Carlos sat together while she helped him knit a couple more rows and then decreed he was doing much better and they should go for a walk and enjoy the night air. Mabel and Clara decided to watch a film in Clara's room and couldn't decide between a new movie or an old one.

After several minutes of dithering, Sylvia coldly suggested that, since they had all night, they had time to watch both films. They cast a glance at her and scuttled away.

Finally, everyone was gone, and only then did Sylvia take me and Gran into her suite of rooms. I'd been here often enough that I no longer marveled at how much like a glamorous film set she kept her private space.

After making sure her door was shut, she took down a Cubist painting she'd been given back in the day. It wasn't a Picasso; it was from the school of. I got the feeling she could have had the real thing and was irked that she hadn't bought a Picasso when his paintings went for about twenty-five bucks. This "school of" guy was never going to hang in a world-famous gallery, but as a cover for a safe, it wasn't bad.

Even though we were all alone, she still glanced around to double-check and then punched in some complicated security code. She opened the safe, and I held my breath. I didn't want to look, but I couldn't help myself. How often does a person get to look inside the safe of a very wealthy vampire?

CHAPTER 2

The contents of that safe were almost as exciting as my imagination had suggested. There was a stack of gold bricks in there, some small chests, envelopes that I suspected contained stock certificates and probably deeds of property, and who knew what else. And then, from the very back, she pulled out a set of jewelry boxes.

Gran and I looked at each other, and I could see my grandmother's eyes dancing with excitement. Sylvia stroked the top of the largest box the way she would a favorite pet and then opened it, stared at the contents with a little smile, and passed it towards me.

I'd expected something fabulous, but even so, I gasped. The necklace was without doubt the most beautiful piece of jewelry I'd ever seen. Yes, I'd seen the Crown Jewels, and I'm not going to pretend that the Koh-i-Noor isn't amazing, but a big, honking diamond the size of an ostrich egg in a crown has a different kind of beauty than a set of jewels designed by Cartier for an actress in the 1920s. It was never meant to denote royalty. This piece was all about glamour in a time when glamour meant something, as Sylvia would be the first to tell you.

It was a necklace of diamonds and strategically placed emeralds. The large emerald was off-center, sort of the way you might tie a bow to the side. Surrounding it were a couple of baguette-cut emeralds, and the whole thing was set in a collar of diamonds that sparkled like nothing I'd ever seen before. I almost felt like I couldn't catch my breath. She seemed quite pleased at my stunned response.

"Lovely, isn't it?"

"I cannot even begin to tell you how beautiful this is."

She put that box down and opened the rest: matching earrings, bracelets for each wrist, and an emerald and diamond ring.

I was overwhelmed. Also panicked.

"Sylvia, I can't go out in public wearing all this stuff. I'd be terrified."

"Naturally, on the night of the gala, we'll drive you in the Bentley and bring you home again afterward. During the gala there will, of course, be tight security. You've nothing to worry about."

My eyes opened wide. "You're coming too?" This seemed like a very bad idea. I glanced at Gran, hoping she could talk Sylvia out of this crazy carpool, but she seemed like she was completely on board.

"It'll be such an adventure. Of course, we won't go to the gala. But we can watch you walk up the red carpet."

"Red carpet?"

"Yes. At St. Peter's College. It's going to be so beautiful."

St. Peter's College was one of the oldest colleges in Oxford, and that was saying something. The earliest part of the college dated back to the middle ages. That much I knew. I'd peeked through the gates when I'd walked by and admired the ancient spire and the gorgeous gardens. Now I was going to enter the gates in a Bentley and walk into the college on a red carpet.

I felt like I was sinking deeper and deeper in quicksand. "How big is this shindig?"

Sylvia looked pained. Those famous eyes half-closed as though the very sight of me was painful to her. "The press and dignitaries as well as influential movie people have been invited."

"I'm not sure I can hang around with a bunch of famous rich people and pretend to be your heir. I'm not an actress."

She stiffened. "You are my heir. Although how you could be when you have so little sense of style is completely beyond me. You will go to the meeting, where you will sign the contracts that I will naturally have looked over first. Then, you'll wear the jewels at the gala."

"What if I trip or something?" I asked in a nervous voice. I was more the jeans and sweater type. She looked me up and down, and I knew she was thinking I was the jeans and sweater type too.

"We've a little time. We must practice."

I didn't like the sound of this. "Practice what?"

"Lucy. If you are going to wear these jewels, you will wear them properly. Now—" She reached out and tilted my chin up. "You've quite a nice neck. Not, of course, as lovely as mine, which was once likened to the stem of a lily, but acceptable if you hold your head up properly. Also, the shoulders. The spine must be lovely and straight. What you really need is a full training in the Alexander Technique, but there isn't time."

"The Alexander Technique?" I'd heard of it but thought it was a style of acting, like the Stanislavski Method.

"Yes. The Alexander Technique is a full regimen that teaches movement and breathwork. It was essential to my acting success. The training might help you to stand and move with more grace."

She was killing me with the compliments.

She studied me. "You'll wear a simple gown. Black, of course, to emphasize the jewels. Your hair won't be exactly the way I wore it when I filmed *The Professor's Wife*. You haven't the bone structure, but I have an idea."

And it was very clear that I wasn't going to have any say in my own appearance for this gala.

"The dressmaker is working on your evening gown now. Your role is quite simple. You will pose. You will smile. You will make sure the jewels are shown off to perfection. You will mingle and say the words I will script for you. And then you will slip away."

Before I could stop her, Sylvia took the beautiful necklace out of the box and placed it around my neck. I could see in her eyes that she didn't want to do it, and she could no doubt see in my eyes that I didn't want her to do it. This was her necklace, her fame and her career, not mine. The necklace felt cool and heavy and foreign around my neck. The earrings hung heavily from my lobes, and when she clasped the two bracelets around my wrists, they felt like shackles. She slipped the ring on last and made a face when she saw the state of my nails. To Gran, she said, "Make a note that she'll need a manicure."

Gran nodded and did as she was bid. I didn't like that the undead movie star was turning my grandmother into a personal secretary, but Gran seemed so thrilled that I didn't say anything. I would have loved to take just one glimpse of what I looked like in a mirror, but of course, down here, there were no mirrors. It would be pointless. Soon enough I'd be able to see what the set looked like on me. No doubt there'd be plenty of photographs snapped at this gala. My mind shied away from that idea.

Sylvia also seemed to be thinking ahead to when I'd be the human mannequin whose only purpose was to display these jewels to advantage. She said in a commanding tone, "Now. Remember what I said." She put her hand on top of my head and plucked at a lock of hair. "There is a rope attached to the top of your head, and it is pulling you gently upward." I felt it, too. Like I was a human puppet. And I knew who was pulling the strings.

Still, I did as she told me and stood straighter. "And the shoulders back," she said. "And the hips slightly forward."

This was like some weird game where you impersonated a robot. That's how I felt, jerking back and forth. I felt extremely uncomfortable, but she nodded. "And now we walk."

I barely prevented myself from rolling my eyes. I was tired, it was after midnight, and I already knew how to walk. However, I had learned with Sylvia that it was easier and quicker to do her bidding. Obligingly, I walked across the living space and back again.

"What?" I asked, seeing her expression.

"It pains me. It absolutely pains me to watch young

women walk these days. Are you hiking a mountain? Are you an explorer in the Arctic on snowshoes?"

I didn't answer her because these were obviously rhetorical questions and not the most polite ones at that. She waved her hand, bending only at the wrist as though she were conducting a ballet. "Light on the feet. We don't march. We glide." And then she demonstrated. She looked magnificent. There was no doubt about it. She walked like a runway model. Or a movie star. But I wasn't a movie star, and I had no pretense to be one. I was an American woman who sold wool for a living and wore hand-knit sweaters. I was struggling enough to knit, never mind glide.

But she pierced me with a steely gaze. "Now do what I just did."

Oh yeah, that was going to happen. I did my best. I imagined this rope was pulling me up. I pushed my shoulders back, my hips forward, took a few jerky steps, and I nearly fell over.

She shook her head. To Gran, she said, "What is this passion among young women to wear boots and trousers and go about looking like men?"

"Times change, Syliva," Gran reminded her gently. "And fashion changes with them."

"Not always for the better."

I might not be an expert in fashion history but I'd take my 'men's clothes' any day over corsets and girdles. However, I wisely kept my mouth shut.

"Never mind, when you get up to your apartment, you must practice on your high heels."

Of course, this torture could only get worse. I couldn't manage to walk across the room looking like her in my comfortable boots. How on earth could I manage in high heels? Besides, I didn't actually own any. I had some low-heeled pumps. That was it. Somehow, I didn't think my pumps would suit Sylvia's plan to turn me into a pale version of her for one night.

"I have to be honest, Sylvia. I don't think I can pull this off."

Her eyes were cold and very hard. That emerald had nothing on her. "You will do it because you promised me you would. And I am relying on you."

I bit my lip. I remembered all the nice things she'd done for me. All the beautiful sweaters she'd knitted, and all the times she'd done my hair and lent me jewelry—not the priceless stuff though—and I weakened. I knew this film remake meant the world to her.

"Okay. But please don't expect miracles. I'll never be you, Sylvia."

She laughed softly. "Naturally. But one must do one's best."

As I went back upstairs, I wondered how I had ever been talked into this mess.

And why did I have this terrible feeling in the pit of my stomach that something was going to go wrong?

CHAPTER 3

"What on earth are you doing?" a cool, critical voice demanded.

I nearly jumped out of my skin. I hadn't heard the bell ring. That wonderful warning bell that told me someone was entering my shop. I'd thought I was all alone with the wools and patterns.

I'd been practicing walking, and of all the people to catch me at it, looking like I was rehearsing for some Milan runway show, did it have to be Margaret Twigg? Margaret was a witch who was my sometime mentor and always sarcastic and rude about it. I wasn't about to tell her about Sylvia and the gala, so I said, "I got bored. It was something I saw on YouTube."

Her piercing, blue eyes lit with sarcastic humor. "Have we been watching weddings? Practicing that glide down the aisle, were you?"

It was better she thought that than the truth. "Something like that."

Her lips curved in a superior smile. Her corkscrewed, gray hair jumped up and down as though it was laughing at me.

"It's usually advisable to have a groom lined up before practicing that walk down the aisle."

Oh, ha ha ha. Little did she know. I could have a wedding with a pretty amazing groom if I wanted one.

The trouble was that marriage with the undead came with a whole set of problems that were a lot more sticky than what to do when you got two identical blenders as wedding presents and didn't want either of them.

"Can I help you with something?" I asked her. I doubted she was here for knitting needles.

"I'm glad you're alone," she said, which immediately made me wish I wasn't. If there was something Margaret Twigg had to tell me that no one else could hear, it was probably something I didn't want to know about. She came closer and dropped her voice. Oh, this was really making me nervous. "It's time for you to choose your athame."

When I looked at her blankly, she added, "Your ceremonial dagger."

I could feel the expression of horror pull my facial muscles into some sort of grotesque mask. "My what?"

"Oh, come on," she snapped. "You can't be that clueless." And then she looked at me. "Well, actually, you can. But I wish you'd try a little harder, Lucy. The athame is an important part of your training."

The word dagger was flashing on and off in my head like a neon sign. I shook my head. "I'm a pacifist. My body is a no-weapons zone."

She regarded me from her sharp blue eyes as though I was being a tedious toddler. "An athame is not a weapon. It's symbolic. Metaphoric, if you like. The athame cuts away lies and reveals the truth. It helps you focus your power and your magic."

Okay, that didn't sound so bad. And there were a lot of times I could use such a tool. I looked at the bag she carried at her side. "Are you going to give it to me now?"

She shuddered and took a step back. "I will never forgive your grandmother for not teaching you even the most basic rudiments of our craft."

And I'd never forgive her for dissing my grandmother every chance she got. I must have looked as steely as I felt, for she backed down and said, "Anyway, that's not the point. I can't give you your athame. No one can. You must choose each other."

I didn't want to choose something with a pointy end that could hurt anyone, ceremonial or not.

She said, "Make sure you've got a few hours free tomorrow morning."

"I have a business to run," I reminded her.

She glanced around the shop, empty but for the two of us. "Perhaps you could tear yourself away. Don't you have staff?"

No doubt she knew very well that on Saturdays I did have help. A couple of students from Cardinal College, Polly and Scarlett, worked Saturday mornings, and they could definitely manage fine without me. Still, I didn't want to make it too easy for her. "I'll see if I can clear my schedule."

"Do. We're going shopping."

"For daggers."

She nodded once.

And then she left. This time I did hear the bells. It sounded to me like they were cheering that she was leaving. I felt like cheering too.

I tried to think of an excuse not to go dagger shopping. I considered feigning illness, telling her I had too much work, that my horoscope was inauspicious, but in the end, it was easier to do what Margaret Twigg wanted me to do. If I got out of it tomorrow, she'd only make my life more miserable until I succumbed. Easier to do it the first time out.

So Saturday morning I left Polly and Scarlett to run Cardinal Woolsey's while Margaret Twigg, my cousin Violet and my great-aunt Lavinia and I went shopping.

Violet drove. I thought at first we were headed for Glastonbury. We were definitely headed in that direction, but Margaret told her to turn off onto one of those country roads so narrow that if a car comes the other way, one of the drivers has to back the car up until there's room to pull over and let the other car pass.

Then we turned into another lane, passed a pub called The Green Man and pulled up in front of an obscure little shop in a tiny village that didn't appear to have a name. It certainly didn't have any road signs or a billboard saying, Welcome to Crazy Magic Town. One minute we were driving along a country road, and the next minute there were cottages and houses and a street of shops and the pub, just like any other village in the Cotswolds.

The shop sign was so old, the hand-painted picture on the wooden sign had faded. I could make out a frog sitting on a globe, or maybe that was supposed to be a crystal ball. The shop was called Eye of Newt.

In the front window was a skull, books of shadows, crystals, feathers and printed spells. A Ouija board packaged like a board game. I hadn't been a witch as long as my companions, but this looked like a cheesy tourist shop. When we walked in and I saw the plastic cauldron that was a fountain with multicolored water spewing up, I was convinced this was more toy store than witch emporium. I began to relax. If we bought something here, no doubt my ceremonial dagger would be plastic and made in China.

A small, wizened man was sitting behind the counter, idly playing with a pack of cards. He glanced up when we entered, with the typical shopkeeper's expression and the words "May I help you?" on his lips. I knew because I was an expert at that very same expression and those very same words, having spoken them probably a hundred times a day. But he barely got past the "May I" when he recognized who was calling. He came forward, deferential, practically bowing at the waist in front of Margaret Twigg. "Mistress, you are most welcome."

"Mistress?" I didn't realize I'd said it aloud until my cousin Violet elbowed me and said, "Shh."

Suddenly, the plastic cauldron and tourist stuff didn't seem so cute and harmless. Margaret Twigg said, "Alphonse Young, may I present Lucy Swift."

He looked at me and took my hand in his dry, leathery ones. I felt the shock of connection, like an electric car being plugged in, and when I glanced up, his eyes were boring into mine. They were peculiar eyes. Muddy brown but with streaks of red in them. I'd never seen a human with that color eyes before. I'd never seen a vampire with that color eyes before either. His eyes seemed to hold mine for an uncomfortably long time before he said, "I have heard of this one."

This one? What was I, a heifer coming to market?

Margaret Twigg, instead of sounding impressed that he knew me, sounded irritated. "No matter what I do, she keeps far too high a profile."

He still held onto my hand. It was like being caressed by a lizard. "She's young yet. But there's great power in this one. If you train her well, she will take your place one day." I yanked my hand out of his. Me, become the head of a coven? Oh, that was never happening.

I glanced up at Margaret Twigg, and she looked irritable but resigned, as though this was bad news she'd already accepted. Well, thanks very much. I felt like saying, "News-flash, not going to happen."

The old man nodded at a stripy-haired girl with a nose ring who wandered by. He said, "These are old friends, Matilda. I'm going to take them in the back room. See that we're not disturbed."

Matilda looked as though she lived on a diet of magic mushrooms. Her eyes were glazed and vacant, but she nodded. "I'll watch the front of the shop."

"Thank you, my dear."

And then, putting his hand on my lower back, he urged me forward. No doubt he was worried I was about to bolt, which was definitely on my mind.

We passed through a door that, like everything else in the front of the shop, looked like it was a stage prop from the Harry Potter movies. It was gothic and arched and made of cheap pressboard painted to look like ancient timber. But when he shut the door behind us and I looked around, I didn't feel like I was on a movie set anymore. I felt like I was in the real house of magic.

A skeleton grinned at me, looking uncomfortably real. Cabinets contained pots and jars of ingredients. Shelves contained cauldrons, pentacles and goblets. Candles of every imaginable color filled a shelf, and below that were the books: spell books, books of shadows, and volumes about the history of the craft.

Margaret Twigg said, "Lucy's here for her first athame."

He smiled as though this was the best news he'd heard in a long time. I thought it was also the kind of smile that would-be frat boys got right before they were led into some hideous initiation ritual they might not survive.

"Come," he said to me, and with a snap of his fingers, a glass case I hadn't seen before lit up. Inside it was a long, black, velvet-lined tray, and there must have been thirty or forty ceremonial daggers laid out. Some were beautiful, intricate and carved with magical symbols or had jewel-encrusted handles. Others were very plain. Some of the blades were long and thin; others were short and wide. It didn't seem like there was a classic style.

Mr. Young stood back and urged the others back too. He said, "Please. Step forward and choose your athame. Take your time. Let the magic come to you."

I liked that idea. I always felt that I was trying to pull out of me the magic everyone told me I had. But to relax and let it come to me was a joyous idea. For the first time since we'd set off on this field trip, I began to breathe properly.

Softly, he said, "When you're ready, point to the two or three that speak to you."

I walked forward and stared into the case. And I was immediately drawn to a beautiful and intricately carved dagger that had a winking purple jewel in its hilt. An amethyst, I thought. But I suspected that it had only drawn me because it was the sparkliest and the prettiest. I let my eyes move on. There were no prices listed, of course. I assumed when choosing one's ceremonial dagger, price was no object. Still, I didn't want to end up with a debt that would take me months to pay off.

I looked at the more humble daggers. But none of them were speaking to me. And then I closed my eyes. I didn't make a fancy spell. I said to myself, "Let the right one come to me."

I opened my eyes, and there it was. One athame looked as though it was sending out some kind of weird glow, but I don't think it was. It was letting me know it was the one. The athame that chose me wasn't the most elaborate or the least. It wasn't the longest or the sharpest, the shortest or the bluntest. It was in the middle. But I could feel my palm tingling and my fingers almost curling of their own accord. It would fit in my hand, I knew it instantly. I didn't think I'd moved a muscle, but the old man came forward.

"You've made your choice." He said it as a statement, not a question.

I looked at him. Why was I always surprised when witches acted like witches? I really needed to get over that. I nodded. Almost as though he was making a joke, he said, "Will you need to see a selection?"

We both knew I wouldn't. I pointed and said, "That one."

He looked at the dagger and at me, and then took a sharp, sidelong glance at Margaret Twigg before he said, "Of course."

He didn't open the top of the cabinet as I'd imagined, but a drawer that slid easily out. And then he didn't pick up the dagger and hand it to me. He said, "Take what is yours."

The words gave me a thrilling sensation that went down my arm and into my dominant hand. I reached for the dagger, and I felt how right this was. I hadn't even finished reaching when the dagger closed the distance between us, jumping out of the case and into my hand.

He nodded, looking pleased. "They have bonded."

From another drawer, he brought out a silk bag and a larger leather bag. He instructed me always to keep the dagger inside the silk bag tucked into the leather one, and on no account was anyone else ever to touch it. I nodded. I already felt protective and a bit princessy about this dagger.

It was mine. I hadn't even wanted one when we'd walked into this shop. Now I felt like it was part of me.

Margaret Twigg looked quite satisfied. She said to the old man, "You'll come to her ceremony?"

He smiled. "Wouldn't miss it."

Ceremony? Nobody told me anything about a ceremony. But I knew better than to argue. Not here, not in front of the nice man.

Lavinia was peering at the pots and glass jars. "I'll have the small bottle of chakra oil, please."

And then we all looked around and stocked up. I bought candles and a guide to using your athame that Margaret pushed on me. "Read up," she said.

Violet bought some crystals that I suspect were part of a spell to attract love, and Margaret Twigg bought a small bottle of black powder and a piece of obsidian.

We went out to the front where the cash business was conducted, and the amount he charged me was less than I'd expected.

When we got out of the shop, Margaret Twigg said, "Well, that wasn't so bad, was it?"

I thought that very much depended on what this ceremony involved. A dagger had a sharp point for a reason, and I was a little bit nervous about what that reason might turn out to be.

When I got home, I put my new dagger carefully away in the closet where I kept all my magic props. Two powerful women in the last two days had forced important possessions on me that I didn't want. I wondered what it meant.

CHAPTER 4

*W*e set off in the Bentley for London bright and early on Monday. Theodore was driving, Gran was riding shotgun, and Sylvia and I were in the back seat. Sylvia had the set of jewels in a bag on her lap and both hands protectively crossed on top of them. I wondered if she'd be able to let them go when the time came for me to wear them to the gala.

I wouldn't be a bit surprised if at the last moment she put them around her own neck and tried to spin some story about being her own heir. Frankly, I'd be really happy if she did that. I didn't like being the patsy who got to wear price-less, uninsured jewels to a public event.

Normally, I'd have expected to be sitting up front with Theodore while the two vampires gossiped in the back, but Sylvia had wanted to rehearse with me yet again on my role. And let there be no misunderstanding, it was a role I was playing.

She even made all of us watch *The Professor's Wife*. It was movie night at the vampire's lair. Okay, maybe I hadn't gone to NYU film school, but I did love movies. And, even taking into account that it was a silent movie in black and white, *The Professor's Wife* turned out to be really corny and hackneyed. And I didn't even get popcorn.

Probably the reason the film was so famous and iconic was Sylvia's performance and, of course, the Cartier jewels. Kind of in the same way that Salvador Dalí's sets helped make *Spellbound* so famous. Well, that and Hitchcock directing.

Whoever directed *The Professor's Wife* was no Hitchcock. When the movie was finished, there was silence, and then Gran said, "That was lovely, dear." As though Sylvia had baked her a cake.

"Lucy?" she asked me, her gaze drilling into me as though she might hit oil.

Lovely was already taken, so I went with, "Your performance made the film. And the jewels were fabulous."

She turned off the projector. "If anyone asks your opinion, you'll remark on my subtle, layered performance. They used to say I could break a heart with one glance from my brilliant eyes. Do you need me to write that down for you?"

"No, I'll remember it. Layered, subtle performance. Heart-breaking eyes."

And now those eyes were looking at me as though they'd break a lot more than my heart if I screwed this up. She'd allowed me to choose my own clothing for the meeting, for which I was grateful.

At least for now I felt like myself. I was wearing my best jeans, flat shoes, a comfortable, white cotton shirt and a gorgeous slouchy sweater in blue that Gran had knitted me. I also wore the diamond necklace that Sylvia had given me.

Perhaps it was a reminder that I was a woman accustomed to more modest jewels. I'd put my hair up into a simple, messy updo, mostly to keep it off my neck.

Theodore took the M25, which was the fastest, most direct route, though not the prettiest. With no traffic, we'd be in London in an hour and a half. On the way, Sylvia explained a bit more about the project. "Rune Films is remaking the film," she informed me. "They're a young company, but they've had some hits. *Alexandra* was a sleeper hit about Queen Alexandra. She married Edward VII, of course, but the movie was mainly about how she began the Red Cross."

"Really?" I made a mental note to see the film.

"Her jewels were quite lovely but nothing, of course, like mine," Sylvia said, clasping her jewels more tightly. I didn't know why she'd brought them along. Maybe for good luck.

"There's a second producer involved. Man Drake films. I don't know so much about them. The head producer there is a man named Simon Dent. He's famously reclusive. Models himself on Howard Hughes, I should think. He's never seen but has deep pockets, both of which make him very popular."

Traffic wasn't too bad, and as we drove into Central London, I got as excited as I always did coming into this beautiful city. The producer's offices were in a high-rise sandwiched between an insurance company and an investment firm in SoHo.

I'd imagined driving to a backlot somewhere as though this were Hollywood, but nobody made movies here. This was where the planning went on. Theodore drew up in front of a Victorian red brick building with white arched windows on the main floor that housed a busy coffee shop.

They wished me luck, and I found the main door and the

nameplate for Rune Films. I pushed the buzzer to be let in and took the elevator to the eighth floor, where Rune Films was located. When the elevators opened, I was greeted by a slim man with thinning, fair hair who looked to be in his early forties.

His gaze immediately went to my neck. Perhaps he'd hoped I'd be wearing the jewels to the meeting. I'd have had to drive a wooden stake through Sylvia's heart and pluck that bag out of her cold, dead hands before that would have happened.

The flicker of disappointment in his pale, blue eyes came and went so quickly I almost could have imagined it. He said, with a boyish smile, "Lucy Swift, I presume?"

I nodded.

"I'm Edgar Smith. I'm Simon Dent's business manager. Mr. Dent runs Man Drake films, you know. We're thrilled to be part of the team. I'll take you in now to meet Annabel Holroy and the rest of the team. Annabel is the creative director, and she's marvelous. You're going to love her. Come this way."

He led me down a hallway, and I glimpsed open cubicles with people working on computers, a few offices where small groups were meeting or a person was on the phone. There were movie posters up on the walls, but other than that, I could have been in an insurance or an investment office.

There were no movie stars rubbing shoulders, no films being made. As we walked along, he said, "It's a little quiet at the moment. We've got a movie in editing in the back suite of rooms over there." He gestured to a hallway that led off from the right-hand side. Then he waved his arm in the left direction. "Accounting is down there, and straight ahead of us are the producers' offices."

"It's very exciting," I said. "I've never been in a movie production office before."

This was true and one of the allowable remarks that Sylvia had cleared for me. He turned to smile at me. "This isn't the exciting part. Wait until the movie premiere. You'll love it. Naturally, you'll have a VIP seat." He dropped his voice to a low murmur so I had to lean closer to hear him. "The producers are putting a lot behind this one. They're very excited. Especially that you were generous enough to lend us the Cartier set."

I smiled, but the primary message I was here to deliver was that while Sylvia was perfectly happy for me to wear the jewels for this gala and to have them photographed for advertising purposes, she would not be letting them out of her hands for some actress to wear during filming. They'd have to make a copy. I doubted very much there would be an issue over that. I couldn't imagine the insurance liability the production company would have to take on to use the real jewels in filming.

He ushered me into a glass-walled conference room, where there were six people already sitting around a table. All of them rose, and Edgar Smith made the introductions. "Lucy Swift," he said, "come and meet Annabel."

Annabel stood up where she'd been sitting at the head of the table and came around to shake my hand. She was in her mid-thirties, I'd guess, and looked both smoothly professional and also as though she wasn't getting enough sleep. There were dark circles under her eyes. Still, she beamed with excitement. "We're so excited about this production.

We're doing everything we can to honor the original. Your"—here she paused as though trying to remember something and then said—"great-aunt? Was Sylvia Strand your great-aunt?"

I smiled back, pleased that we'd done so much rehearsing. "Not an aunt by blood," I said, following the script. "Sylvia was a cousin, but my grandmother was her favorite cousin, and so her estate passed through my grandmother to my mother to me."

I didn't know how he'd done it, but Theodore had managed, with the help of Hester and Sylvia's undead lawyer, to create a nonexistent ancestry line from Sylvia to me, and there was paperwork filed where paperwork ought to be in case anyone bothered to check. The truth was, Sylvia had never left her goods to anyone. She still had them.

She nodded and tapped herself lightly on the side of the head. "I have a newborn at home. My brain is mush."

Edgar Smith chuckled softly. "Annabel's mush brain would be anyone else's steel-trap mind."

She shook her head at his flattery and made the rest of the introductions.

Beside her was Bryce Teddington, who was introduced as the accountant for the project. He was lean and nervous. His wispy, black hair was in a bad comb-over that he'd glued to his scalp with Brylcreem. He wore glasses, which enlarged his eyes to almost cartoon-character proportions. He seemed to be muttering to himself, and even sitting, he stooped.

A young woman about my age was a production assistant named Emma. She was tall and slim, with long brown hair, big brown eyes. One of those people who look effortlessly gorgeous. Finally, I met an executive producer, Peter. They all had last names, but I soon gave up trying to remember them. If I tried to remember everyone's first names, I had a chance. Name cards would have been even better. I saw the quick glance they all gave to my neck the same way Edgar Smith had. But no one mentioned my lack of bling. I was invited to sit at the opposite end of the table and offered coffee, tea, water, juices, and even champagne, had I wanted it. I chose a coffee. Anything to keep me sharp.

I supposed I'd fallen into the trap of thinking that movie people would be as glamorous as movie stars. What I'd discovered, if this company was typical of most, was that the glamour was on one side of the screen and the people who made it happen on the other side of the screen. The dull side.

We made small talk, but it all centered around the movie. Mostly it was a bit of a sales pitch. Annabel outlined first how excited they were to be remaking this amazing film. "It was one of the movies they taught us in film school." She glanced at the ceiling and then down to the tabletop. And then, almost as an afterthought, she said, "When I got my master's in Film Studies at NYU."

"That's cool," I said. No doubt she expected me to jump in with some anecdote about my Ivy League education, but I kept my mouth shut. I didn't think my two years of business college was going to impress this bunch.

They went over the contract, which sounded like what Sylvia had already agreed on, and then shifted to what would happen at the gala. "It's our way of jumping up and down and saying, Look at us! We're remaking this classic with things the original didn't have," Annabel said.

"Like sound," Peter added, and everyone laughed.

"Yes, that, of course, but also movies weren't made on

location then as they are now, and we're very excited to work with St. Peter's College in Oxford, which will be our main setting. That's why we're having the gala there."

I tried to look enthusiastic, but I'm not sure I did very well.

Annabel said, "You'll be the guest of honor, of course. And you'll wear the Cartier set."

"Yes. Only for that one night, though. It's in the contract, I believe, that you'll make a replica for the filming."

"Oh, goodness, yes." She waved her hand in front of her face. "Imagine if we lost it or something. It's irreplaceable."

"It is."

She glanced at her notes. "Are you comfortable in front of cameras?"

Oh, that answer was a resounding no, but I had been part of a TV show at my knitting shop with the famous designer Teddy Lamont, and I'd discovered that after the first ten minutes of being super nervous, I'd mostly forgotten about the cameras. There had been a murder during the course of the shooting, but that wasn't relevant.

Besides, if I said "No," I might be offered coaching, and I'd had enough of that with Sylvia. "Yes," I said. "I think I can handle it."

She nodded. "You know not to look at the camera unless directed to do so?"

I nodded. Even if I wasn't a natural, Sylvia had been very clear about how to act as though there was no camera pointing at me.

A worried frown creased her brow. "And you know not to talk about politics or anything remotely controversial? There will be loads of media there, and we want to keep our remarks to positive comments about the production."

I nodded again. Imagine if I told the world that Sylvia walked the earth still, even if she wasn't still alive. That would certainly get this movie some attention.

But of course I didn't. We went through the sequence of events for the evening, since they clearly assumed I hadn't read all the briefing notes they'd already sent me. In fact, I'd practically memorized them and been quizzed by Sylvia.

"Great," she said brightly. "All that's left for you to do now is sign the contract."

The assistant, Emma, brought it and placed it in front of me, giving me a beautiful pen with the production company's logo on it. She said, "That's yours to keep. Call it a good-luck charm."

The nervous accountant said, "Don't forget to read the contract, which you should always do before signing one. Especially sections—"

"Yes, yes," the producer interrupted. "Lucy's not a fool."

And yet they had shoved a contract in front of me open to the signing page. I glanced up at the nervous accountant and thought he was trying to send me a message. Or was it just that his eyes were so magnified by the glasses that it looked like he was trying to tell me something? Still, I didn't want to be a fool.

"I assume this is the same contract my lawyer looked over?" And what they didn't know was that Sylvia had already read over this contract, but it wouldn't be a bad idea for me to give it a quick glance over too. Sylvia hadn't been in the business for decades now, and I did have that two years of business college.

I flipped back to the first page. I could feel everyone in the room watching me. No doubt they had other, much more important things to do than watch me read over a boring contract. I wanted to tell them to go on. I didn't need them in the room. But I supposed politeness held them hostage.

It was as dull as any other contract I'd ever read. Not that there'd been that many. As Sylvia's heir, I agreed that her likeness could be used for promotional purposes. And then the section about the jewelry I was lending. That, I read more carefully. It seemed very straightforward though. At the end, I did look up. "This seems clear that you only get the jewelry for the gala. And I'm agreeing that for the filming itself, you'll be using a copy."

The producer said, "Oh, yes. Can you imagine what our insurance costs would be if we were using a one-of-a-kind Cartier jewelry set during filming?" She shuddered visibly. "I can't even do that math. Definitely. We only want you wearing the real thing for the launch party. There'll be security everywhere. You won't be alone for a minute. Nothing can go wrong."

I nodded, but somehow I didn't feel completely relieved. It was amazing how often when someone said nothing can go wrong that something immediately did.

CHAPTER 5

$\mathcal{I}$ read the rest of the contract, but it all looked fine to me. Sylvia and her estate weren't taking on any liability and they weren't attempting to use her jewelry, so I thought I'd grasped enough of that contract to be confident to sign. Which I did.

The minute my pen lifted from the page, Emma took the contract to Peter. I heard a sound like a gunshot. I jumped in my seat only to realize that someone had popped a bottle of champagne. We each had a small glass while Annabel made a toast.

"To *The Professor's Wife.* Let's hope her second marriage is even more successful than her first."

We all laughed and then sipped. I didn't hang around much longer. It was pretty clear they all had things to do. As I was leaving, Edgar Smith said, as he escorted me once more to the elevator, "I understand you live in Oxford. I'll be driving down. Would you like me to pick you up for the gala? You know I'd be only too happy to."

I was touched and grateful. I actually would have liked

him to pick me up. It would have been nice to walk up that terrifying red carpet on the arm of somebody who knew a few people, but Sylvia had been very clear that I would be driven in the Bentley. I and the jewels would only be outside of her jurisdiction for the shortest possible time. So I turned to him and said, "Thank you so much. I already have my ride planned. But I hope you'll look out for me and introduce me to a few people?"

He understood immediately what I meant. "Of course. There's nothing worse than being pitchforked into a room full of strangers. But don't worry, you'll be the guest of honor. The belle of the ball, may I say. I'm sure your dance card will be full the entire evening."

He shook my hand as I left, and I was so pleased I had at least one friendly face to look out for at the gala.

And I had until Friday to perfect learning to walk!

However, it turned out our London trip wasn't complete. There was a visit to a fashion designer in Belgravia. It was so exclusive, we had to ring the bell to be let in. Naturally, I had no say in the gown I was to wear. Sylvia had already been working with the designer by phone and email, so all I was here for was a fitting.

The dress was simplicity itself. A long, figure-hugging column of black, strapless with a sweetheart neckline. Not a bow or a flounce or a speck of decoration marred its simplicity. Essentially, I would be the human equivalent of the black silk that lined the jewelry cases that housed her fabulous collection.

She'd sent them my measurements, and when I tried it on, the dress—or was it, officially, a gown?—only needed to be hemmed. They were waiting for me to stand in it wearing the correct shoes. A selection was before me. Each had a higher heel than I'd ever worn before and, like the dress, was simple, black and strappy. The third pair fit the best, but I felt like I was walking on stilts. However, I was a good sport and stood patiently while the designer's helper pinned the hem. Delivery was promised for Thursday.

This was getting real.

Naturally, when the dress arrived Thursday, it was perfect.

Friday, I wasn't allowed to work in my own shop. I had a full day of facial, nails—both hands and feet—and makeup and hair. Sylvia sent a photo of the hairstyle and instructions for the makeup, which was relatively light. The stylist did my hair in a slightly complicated knot at the back of my neck that left my neck and ears bare.

We'd agreed that I'd dress in my flat, as the thought of navigating the tunnels and the rough wooden steps beneath my flat in those heels was more than I could cope with. Sylvia agreed, and she and Gran arrived at six to help me dress. I'd grabbed a sandwich at the covered market after my hair appointment, as I knew I wouldn't have time for dinner.

She cast a critical eye over everything, from my French-polished toes to the crown of my head, before helping me to slip into the dress and the new underwear she'd bought to go under it. She must have known I had nothing this nice in my wardrobe.

While it was kind of fun to play dress-up, I felt the weight of responsibility to someone I both liked and admired and was a bit scared of.

At last, she opened the magic jewel boxes and placed the pieces on me herself. When she slipped the diamond necklace around my neck, I shivered. Partly it was the cold platinum against my skin and partly nerves.

When she'd placed the earrings, bracelets and ring on, she stood back and narrowed her eyes as though searching for a flaw. Finally, after Gran and I stood waiting without daring to speak or breathe, she nodded. "Yes. That will do."

It wasn't wild praise, but at least I could breathe again.

"Theodore will drive you in the Bentley, and he will pick you up again precisely at ten o'clock."

"I won't forget."

I snuck a peek in the mirror, and I had to admit, Sylvia knew what she was doing. I barely saw myself at all. The jewels dominated. Sparkle, style, elegance. I could see why vintage Cartier cost so much. From the luster of the jewels to the design, the pieces were exquisite.

When my door buzzer went, Sylvia said, "That will be Theodore with the car." However, when we got downstairs, I found not only Theodore standing there looking uncomfortable but Rafe.

He looked down at Sylvia coldly. "I will drive Lucy."

Sylvia was not happy with this change in her careful planning but it was clear from his tone and expression that Rafe had made up his mind. She looked as though she were going to argue, then settled on, "You know you can't go in? Not only will there be cameras there, but, due to the tight security, no one can attend the party who isn't on the guest list."

"You're saying Lucy, who is the guest of honor, can't bring an escort?"

Sylvia put her chin forward. "She opted not to."

One hundred percent not true. Sylvia hadn't given me the

option. However, I didn't challenge her. I was going to be nervous enough. If I had to worry about Rafe getting caught on camera or hovering over me like an overprotective vampire, I'd be even more of a wreck.

He said, "If Lucy goes at all, I will drive her."

"You can't so much as get out of the car. This has all been arranged. She'll be helped out of the car and escorted down the red carpet by an executive producer."

Another silent tug of wills ensued and he said, "Very well." I was relieved to have Rafe drive me and thankful Sylvia had been talked out of coming in the car with us.

He held the back door open and, with a last glance at Gran, who nodded encouragingly, I got in the car.

"Don't crease that dress," were Sylvia's last words.

Fortunately, it wasn't a long drive. Rafe said, "Is this really something you want to do?"

First, it was pretty late to be changing my mind, and second, now that the event was happening, I found I did. I was suddenly reliving childhood dreams where Cinderella gets to go to the ball after all. Sylvia and Gran weren't exactly fairy godmothers, but they had transformed me from plain Lucy Swift who ran a knitting shop to a glamorous woman going to a fancy party. I remembered as a kid practicing my acceptance speech at the Oscars, waving to the crowds from the red carpet. For one night, I was living my childhood dream. So I could honestly answer, "Yes. Sylvia's done a lot for me. I'm happy to do her a favor."

He made a sound low in his throat. "Sylvia usually gets what she wants."

I didn't answer, as arguing was pointless. We both knew he was right.

The Bentley drove through the gates of St. Peter's College in Oxford, as prearranged by magical movie people, and the moment I had been dreading and anticipating was here.

To the paparazzi and the movie producers, it might look like part of a publicity stunt, but this Bentley wasn't a hired car, and the driver wasn't some out-of-work actor with a chauffeur's cap on his head. When I looked in the rearview mirror, no one looked back, but when the driver turned his head, I saw Rafe staring back, and my nerves died down.

He said, "Remember, any trouble at all, just call my name and I'll hear you."

I nodded.

He moved as though he'd get out of the car then must have remembered he couldn't. Instead, the movie's executive producer, Peter Lambert, was waiting, very dapper in a tux, and opened the door himself. I could hear Sylvia's words in my head, we'd practiced this so many times. *Take your time, one foot out, then take the outstretched hand and come forward in a smooth move right to standing.* I remembered to breathe as she'd taught me. I was so nervous I thought I might stumble on the unfamiliar high heels, but I had a little magic in me. The Alexander Technique was great, but so was a spell.

I was nothing but a living mannequin to display the jewelry. And I felt it. I could feel the flash and sparkle at my neck and wrists and ears. I stopped and posed as Sylvia had taught me to do while photographers snapped pictures and a movie camera filmed the entrance.

The producer said, "This is marvelous. We've got such a good turnout. Of course, we spared no expense, hiring the best public relations team in London. This movie will be a sensation."

"That's wonderful," I said. My job was simply to mouth inanities. Sylvia had warned me that nobody wanted to see my personality or hear my opinions. I was only here to showcase the jewels. If she could have put duct tape over my mouth, she'd have been pleased to do it. Instead my lips were covered with an unfamiliar layer of lipstick.

I managed to make it down the red carpet without tripping over my feet. I tried to remember to hold my head high and my shoulders back and my hips forward and to smile and not look at the camera, and it was like writing a math test. So many variables, most of which I didn't even understand, and trying to make sense of the whole pattern. But somehow I managed.

Peter led me through the huge gothic stone archway, where the doors had been thrown open, and into a stone-floored entranceway with a broad stone staircase going up. But he turned me to the right and into a grand hall of some kind. Again, the floors were flagstone, the walls pale stone, pillars fanned out to an intricate carved ceiling far, far above. I felt as though the whole space had been designed to show off Sylvia's jewels. No paintings took the eye. Only the lovely, medieval arched windows added atmosphere. A lot of people seemed to be gathered here, all glamorous in their designer finery.

Against one wall, a large screen played the original *The Professor's Wife*. It was jarring seeing a much younger Sylvia on screen. Even though the movie was in black and white, the jewels still looked remarkable.

The waiters wandering around with trays were all dressed in 1920s period costume, the men in spats with slicked-back hair and dark suits, the women in flapper gowns and bobbed hair.

I'd make sure Sylvia got some photos of this. She'd have loved to be here.

Peter handed me off to Annabel, the creative director, who'd obviously been on the lookout for me.

"Lucy," she said in a gushing tone, her eyes zeroing in on the necklace, "you look fabulous."

The British have a way of saying words like "fabulous" that makes each syllable sound like two. Still, I was happy to be fabulous. At least for tonight. She didn't need to know that my feet were hurting in the unfamiliar high heels, or that Sylvia had sprayed so much hairspray in my hair that I felt like I was wearing a bicycle helmet, or that the underwired, strapless bra was digging into me in places that made it hurt to breathe. Sylvia had said, when she'd finished, "You'll do." In Sylvia speak, that was pretty close to Annabel gushing "fabulous."

And in order to get through the evening, I simply imagined I was Sylvia. Whenever someone said something to me, I would interpret it in my head and think, "What would Sylvia say or do?"

Although I had to amend that. "What would Sylvia say or do if she was in a good mood and trying to impress you?" That got rid of the sarcasm and the cutting remarks. For the most part.

Edgar Smith, Man Drake's business manager, was as good as his word, and I soon found him at my elbow.

"How are you holding up?" he asked me.

"I'm all right. A bit intimidated."

He nodded. "Just so you know," he said in a low, intimate

tone, "the ladies' room is through the arch in the far corner on the right-hand side. I'll make sure that the first three people you meet are the most important ones, and after that they're all about the same."

I was so grateful to him, I almost sagged with relief. Except that I wasn't allowed to sag. I had that imaginary rope pulling the top of my head into the correct puppet pose. He picked up my hand, and I thought he was going to squeeze it for reassurance, but instead he looked at the emerald and diamond ring on my finger. "That is one serious piece of bling," he said.

I giggled. "I know. Isn't it gorgeous? It's heavier than I thought it would be."

He looked puzzled. "Don't you ever wear that set?"

First, I hadn't even known it existed until a couple of weeks ago. But, even if it was mine, I doubted I'd ever wear it. I now understood why Sylvia had insisted I do nothing but mouth platitudes. I'd already said something stupid. To recover, I basically told him the truth. "I'm afraid something will happen to the set. It's priceless. What if I lost it or it got stolen? I'd never forgive myself."

He seemed quite puzzled by that. "But they're yours. You can do whatever you want with them." He shook his head at me. "If they were mine, I'd hang them around my girlfriend's neck. Then I could look at them all the time."

I supposed it was like Rafe and his fabulous paintings that he kept in his manor house. Sure, they were incredibly valuable, but he kept them around because he loved to look at them.

Keeping my hand in his, Edgar led me forward. Before we reached the person he was leading me to, he said in a low tone, "Lord Alan Pevensy. He's got deep pockets and enjoys funding films, so make sure you fawn over him."

I nodded. And then suddenly I was standing in front of a gray-haired man with bright, brown eyes, the top of whose head just about reached the tip of my nose in my high heels. Edgar made the introductions, and Sir Alan said, "Well, what a pleasure this is. I'm a big fan of your great-aunt's films. She was a radiant delight, and I can see that you are too. You definitely take after her. Have you thought about a career on screen, my dear?"

I recognized the practiced flirtation, but I also liked him. For about a quarter of a second I imagined jumping at his offer. Throwing myself into the glamorous world of acting. And that was long enough. I said, "Actually, I own a knitting shop."

He raised his eyebrows at that. "A knitting shop. How charming." Weirdly, he didn't sound patronizing. "That must be why you look so wholesome. And fresh. The truth is, the life of a professional actress isn't always a happy one. You're much better off where you are."

I heartily agreed. I thought if I had to do very many more of these kinds of evenings, I'd not only be bored stiff but crippled from high heels, and my lungs might be permanently damaged from the underwire of this bra.

Lord Pevensy introduced me to his wife, Lady Pevensy, who was about my height and about my age. She was nice enough, though she did say, "Al, can't you buy vintage Cartier for me?" And she ran her finger across the jewels around my neck.

Her husband laughed heartily. "Couldn't afford it, my

dear. Unless you want to skip private school for our children," and he winked at me.

Naturally, she fell for it. She turned to him. "Really, Alan. You're so rich, you could afford both."

"Not the way you spend money, my dear."

Edgar tugged gently on my arm, and I was very happy to escape from the gently squabbling couple. Even though it looked like a practiced argument, I didn't want to be part of it. Besides, my job was to circulate.

Show off the bling.

CHAPTER 6

To my surprise, the next person Edgar introduced me to was someone I knew. She was a customer of mine. Patricia Beeton. "Patricia is the costume designer," he told me. "She's very much hoping that you might have pictures of Sylvia that aren't in the public domain. Anything from her private albums would be a help."

Patricia Beeton wore the most gorgeous, long, deco gown. It was remarkable to me because it was hand-knitted. Though I recognized the wool, I hadn't sold it to her, so hadn't known she'd be here tonight or even that she was attached to this movie. The dress was black with silver geometric patterns down the front.

"Lucy. I'm so glad I was able to wear something I made from the wools I buy at your shop."

"Honestly, I can't believe how beautifully that turned out," I said, standing back to take in the full view. She'd gone all out, styling her hair in a bob and wearing a velvet headband with a feather in it.

She looked really pleased by the compliment. "Few people understand how much glamour one can achieve knitting with the right wools."

There was a lot more to it than that, as I knew well. It was also the talent of the knitter. And Patricia Beeton could rival any of my vampires in skill. She shook her head at me. "You should be wearing one too, Lucy. What a wonderful way for you to advertise your shop."

I smacked my forehead as though it was a great idea and I'd been too foolish to think of it. In truth, Sylvia would never have let me wear anything that took the eye away from the Cartier set. I and the dress I was wearing were merely here to show the jewels off to their best advantage. Well, second best advantage, as Sylvia would no doubt think.

She waved her hand, and one of the photographers came over. "We'll get a photograph together. I'll make sure you get a copy so you can put it in your newsletter."

I told her that was a great idea, and we posed together for a shot.

When that was done, she turned to me. "I really want to be as true to the original film as possible. We're not going to copy the costumes, but I want to pay homage to Sylvia Strand, who wasn't only a great actress but a fashion icon in her day."

I'd have to remember to pass that compliment on.

"Any photos you can find of her would help. I want to capture her look as much as I can for the costumes."

I had a sneaking suspicion that Sylvia probably had a lot of photographs and personal memorabilia. I said, perfectly honestly, "There are all kinds of Sylvia's things I haven't even looked at. I'll definitely go through them for you. I know Sylvia would be thrilled to see you taking such care to be authentic."

A waiter who looked like an extra in *The Great Gatsby* came by with a silver tray of champagne and sparkling water and red and white wine to choose from. Naturally, I chose champagne. Well, Sylvia had told me to take the champagne, as it would suit the outfit the best. She'd even trained me in how to hold it so that my wrist was cocked in a way that displayed the bracelet the best. I saw it catch the light and sparkle. It really was the prettiest set. As I began to relax, I started to enjoy myself. It was like playing dress-up, only instead of my mother's silk dressing gown and her costume jewelry, I was wearing genuine, priceless jewels, in a genuine, designer gown, with genuine, killer high heels that had to have been designed by a man.

Annabel gently pried me away from Patricia Beeton and led me to an important entertainment reporter next. Again, under Sylvia's orders, I barely sipped the champagne. I only held it as a prop while she asked me questions like, "How does it feel to see *The Professor's Wife* being remade?"

Of course I couldn't tell her that I hadn't seen the original until recently. "I'm very excited. I know that Sylvia would be so honored to see the care and attention the production company is taking to keep the remake both authentic and updated."

She nodded. No doubt she'd read the same words in a press release. "And how do you feel? Wearing a set of jewels that were designed by Jacques Cartier himself? He designed for Elizabeth Taylor and Wallis Simpson, to name only two."

For once I didn't go with the scripted words Sylvia had given me to say. I went with the truth. "Honestly? I'm terrified. They're so exquisite and so beautiful and so expensive."

Suddenly she smiled, a much more natural smile, and leaned in. Now we were just two girls talking. Although I was never not aware that she was recording us. "I know. I'd be terrified too. Can I touch them?"

I laughed. "Of course." I held out the hand that wasn't holding the champagne, and she moved the bracelet on my wrist so that it caught the light and sparkled. Not to be outdone, the ring flashed too.

"They're magnificent," she said, touching the cool stones.

"I think so too."

She asked me a few more standard questions and then had her picture taken with me. From the corner of my eye, I saw the accountant, Bryce Teddington, hovering. He didn't look any more confident or commanding now than he had in the office. He was thin and stooped and nervous. He was biting his nails, watching me the way a hungry puppy might watch its master making dinner.

I smiled at him in an encouraging way, and he stepped forward. That was the signal for the entertainment reporter to head on her way. She said, "I'd better go. I'm trying to catch tonight's deadline."

Bryce glanced nervously left and right. Maybe he'd been told not to monopolize the woman flashing the fancy jewels for the press. He was muttering before he was close enough for most people to hear him. I have exceptional hearing; I've never been sure if it's part of my magic or just one of those freak accidents of birth. "Where's the director? Where are the stars?" he was mumbling. Poor little man. Had he come here hoping to meet celebrities?

Then he came up to me. "I'm not sure you understood the contract thoroughly," he said in a low, nervous tone.

I was a bit concerned. "What do you mean?" Wasn't he supposed to be on their side?

"Balance sheet's not adding up. Debits don't match credits. You see?" His eyes were magnified like a huge bluebottle's, and it made it hard to concentrate on his words.

"I've never been too good with numbers. I'm not really following." And surely there were other people I was supposed to be chatting with. Not the company accountant.

"Balance sheet. Such an elegant concept. Balance. But when something's out of balance, it tips the scale, do you see?"

I knew I should move on, but he seemed very determined to make me understand something. "I think you need to explain this to me in a way I can grasp." Like if he spoke English rather than Spreadsheet.

He looked past me and jumped like a frightened, cornered rabbit. "Not here."

"But my lawyer went over the whole thing. I don't understand what the problem is."

Again, he said in that low, nervous voice, "Not here. Meet me—" And then he stopped talking. It was pretty clear that he hadn't come up with an idea of where I should meet him. The poor man. He was so nervous. He glanced around and finally said, "Make your way to the ladies' powder room."

I raised my eyebrows. "You're going to meet me in the ladies'?" Oh, that was hardly going to raise eyebrows.

He shook his head impatiently. "Past the ladies', there's a

small waiting room. No one knows it's there. In fifteen minutes. Meet me there. I've got something I must tell you. Discrepancy. Important."

When an accountant talked about discrepancies, I had to assume the budget wasn't adding up. I felt for him, but Sylvia and I had nothing to do with the film's finances. She—or her estate—were getting a fee for her likeness and the use of the jewels, but Sylvia wasn't in this for money. For Sylvia, this was an ego trip down memory lane.

I thought he was a bit of a crackpot, but he was clearly concerned. I should at least hear him out. Meeting by the bathroom was strange, but he was obviously harmless and besides, within fifteen minutes, I probably would need a trip to the ladies' to adjust my underwire.

I nodded. "All right." And then before I could say another word, he disappeared. Just melted away.

Annabel came up with a man I recognized. He was a movie star. One of those famous British ones that's always in romantic comedies. Darkly good looking, with a big, toothy grin and floppy hair. Before he was introduced, he said, taking my hand, "I was hoping you were my co-star. You're gorgeous. There might be love scenes, you know. Are you sure you won't have a go?"

I gave a nervous giggle, and Annabel said, "Oh, stop it, Adrian. Lucy's got better things to do than flirt with you."

Though, at the moment, I couldn't think what they might be. It wasn't every day a girl got hit on by a movie star. Well, not this girl.

She said, "We've talked Adrian into taking the lead in *The Professor's Wife.*"

Oh, I thought Sylvia would be very pleased with that

choice. "That's great." I looked around. "But who's playing the wife?" Sylvia would be much more interested to find out who was portraying her part. She'd be the star of the show, after all.

She tapped the side of her nose like a secret agent. "That's going to be our next big reveal."

She excused herself and walked away, and Adrian leaned in and dropped his voice, "That means they haven't got anybody yet."

"They've got you."

He shrugged. "I came cheap because I just got out of rehab. We all know it will be the female lead who carries this thing."

I was still taking in the fact that he was so honest about being in rehab. He seemed to be the only lead actor here, and by his own admission, he'd come cheap. I wondered if Bryce Teddington was on to something with his nervous questions. "Who's directing the film?" I asked Adrian.

He tilted his extremely gorgeous head to one side, then said, "Don't think one's attached to the project, yet."

Then he looked past me and said, "Oh, excuse me, I must say hello to Lord Pevensy."

Clearly he had his own agenda being here, no doubt to suck up to the power people. I didn't blame him. I wished him well and then, before he left, I asked him the time. Naturally, I wasn't wearing a watch, and Sylvia hadn't allowed me to bring my cell phone. He gave me the time. Nearly fifteen minutes had gone by since I'd had that bizarre message from Bryce.

I made my slow and decorous way towards the ladies'

room. I was stopped two or three times for a picture and a murmur of appreciation about the fabulous jewels I was wearing.

I slipped down the corridor. It was so quiet, I could hear the silk of my dress rustle and my shoes tap the stone floor. The lighting was discreet. Even the word ladies' in tastefully subtle brass letters. I was so glad that Edgar had pointed it out to me when I'd first arrived or I never would have found it. I passed an alcove with an antique table with a lamp on it, and then to the left, another alcove held the door to the ladies'. This opened as I grew close, and a young flapper came out. I pretended to be going into the bathroom until she was out of sight, then continued on my way.

The elegance ended the second I got past the bathroom, though. It seemed like I was heading to the working part of the college. A laundry cart was pushed against the wall with dirty linens piled high.

I glanced quickly behind me, feeling like I was doing something furtive, and then I kept going. The accountant had been right. There was nobody down here.

I wondered how he had even known there was this little cloakroom or whatever it was. But sure enough, there was a small sitting room to the right. Two couches, side tables with lamps. There was no one in there. I was either the first or he'd forgotten all about me or played some stupid trick.

I couldn't wait down here when I was specifically at this event to show off Sylvia's Cartier set. I'd been happy to indulge him for a couple of minutes and find out what was worrying him so much, but I couldn't linger.

I heard something. Felt something. I didn't know what. I

turned to look behind me when something hit me on the back of the head. Hard.

Lightning exploded in the front of my vision, and then everything went dark.

CHAPTER 7

I opened my eyes and then immediately closed them again on a wince. My head was splitting, and the light hurt them.

"Don't try to move. You're all right." The commanding voice immediately soothed me.

"Rafe," I said weakly. Never had I been so happy to hear his voice. His cool, capable hands touched my head gently.

"Ouch," I cried when he touched a particularly sore spot on my head.

I didn't know where I was. Why I was lying on the floor. Or why there were so many people around me. I felt sick and disoriented. I just wanted to lie quietly in the dark.

A voice I vaguely recognized was saying, "Is she all right? Is she still alive?"

It was a woman's voice. I'd heard it recently. What was her name?

"Annabel," I said, pleased my brain was working that well. She must have thought I'd called for her, for the movie producer knelt down beside me. "Lucy. I can't believe you were attacked. Here at our lovely party. Are you all right?"

What did she think? I was lying on the floor in pain. Of course, I wasn't all right. Before I could think of the words to make her go away, Rafe took control. "Lucy's been injured. She can't talk at the moment."

It all came rushing back, and I immediately put my hand to my throat. I felt that my skin was clammy and my pulse was racing. But where was the necklace?

I was all but clawing at myself trying to find the thing. I looked at my wrist. It was empty. Even that ring was gone.

I tried to lift my head, but Rafe put a gentle hand on my forehead and said, "Lie still. There's a doctor coming."

"The jewels," I said. "Do you have them?" It was a faint hope.

He said, "Lucy, the jewels have been stolen."

For a nanosecond, I wished whoever had attacked me had hit me a lot harder so that I wouldn't have to face Sylvia.

In hardly any time, a doctor was bending over me. And then I was allowed to get up. I was glad of this because there's something so humiliating about lying on the floor when people are standing over you, staring. Rafe helped me to my feet and put an arm around me to prevent me from sagging back to the floor.

Someone stepped forward. "The police are here."

He shook his head. "Later. Lucy needs medical attention. They can speak to her tomorrow."

"Tell them," I said to Rafe. "Tell them they have to find the jewels. Sylvia's jewels."

"I will," he said soothingly. "Don't worry. Your only job is to get well."

The doctor gave him some soft-voiced instructions, and then we took a few staggering steps forward. With a soft oath, he leaned down and, putting his arm under my knees, hoisted me up. On a normal day, I would have been quite pleased to be carried around like Scarlett O'Hara, but I was sick, not only from being banged over the head but the horror of what had happened.

Sylvia's precious jewels had gone missing.

On my watch.

I WAS CARRIED DRAMATICALLY through the gala, and as we reached the door, an ambulance pulled up. There were paramedics and a stretcher. And vaguely I realized they had to be for me. I tried to shake my head, but it hurt too much.

"No. I don't want to go to the hospital. I'm fine."

"You're not fine," the doctor said. "I want to check you out properly. You took quite a bang on the back of your head. You could have a fracture."

I almost hoped I did, then maybe Sylvia wouldn't be too angry with me.

It was a faint hope.

I was lifted carefully onto the stretcher by two paramedics and then tucked up in what felt like a blanket. I closed my eyes because the light hurt them. And Rafe kept his hand in mine and we were on our way. I heard someone say in an angry voice, "But I must leave. I can't be held hostage here because of some petty thievery."

That was Lady Pevensy. I recognized her voice. And Edgar, in a soothing voice said, "I'm sorry. I know it's an annoyance, but you must understand something priceless has gone missing. The police have been called. No one can leave until they get here."

Lord Pevensy spoke up now. "I'm not nobody, you know, young man."

"I know that, Your Lordship. I couldn't be more sorry. Please, have patience."

They must have seen me then, because Lord Pevensy made a sound of distress. "Oh, that poor girl. Is she dead?"

And thanks for that. "No, no. Badly injured though."

"Seemed like such a nice young woman. What is this world coming to when thieves and bullies can find their way into a gala at my old Oxford college, eh? That wouldn't have happened in my day."

I closed my eyes then and drifted off.

When I opened them again, I was in the hospital. I was taken for a CT scan and then returned to a room to await the results. Rafe was there. Gran was sitting on the other side of the bed, and I could see she'd been there for a while. Her face was crinkled with concern.

"Lucy. My poor love. How do you feel?"

I looked around. Sylvia wasn't in the room. "Sick."

"Should I call a nurse? Are you going to be ill?"

I shook my head, then winced. "No. I feel sick that the jewels went missing. I don't know what happened."

"You're not to worry about that, my dear. What matters is you."

"Is Sylvia very angry?"

I could see the look they exchanged. It told me everything I needed to know. After an awkward moment, Gran said,

"She's upset about the jewels, of course. But she's as happy as I am that you weren't worse hurt."

"I think I fell into a trap. I didn't mean to. I thought I was doing the right thing. But the accountant, he said he had something important to tell me. I only went down the hallway just past the ladies' bathroom. It wasn't like I met him in a dark alley or anything. I would have thought my magic would have protected me. But it didn't."

"No, dear. It didn't."

"We have to find them."

There was a terrible pain in my head but worse was that awful feeling in my gut that I'd done something unforgiveable. I put my hand to my throat as though Sylvia's priceless and irreplaceable jewels might suddenly appear under my fingertips. But, of course, they didn't. I didn't even care that my head felt like a cracked egg. For all I knew, my brains were leaking out. But I'd happily lose half my brains than have to face Sylvia and tell her I had lost the Cartier set.

A doctor came in and asked me a bunch of foolish questions. What my name was, what the date was, who the prime minister was. I said, feeling irritable and cheeky, "I'm American. We have a president."

But the doctor treated me as I suppose one treats a patient with a concussion. He nodded, looking very serious.

"And do you know who the president is?"

I actually had to think about it for a minute. But I did manage to come up with names of both the president and the prime minister.

He nodded, looking neither pleased nor displeased.

"Can I go home?"

"Yes. Your scan was clear. But I want you to take it very easy. If you start seeing double or can't remember things or the headache gets worse, you're to come back. Do you understand?"

"I do." I matched him for seriousness.

"And I want to see you in my surgery in a week."

I nodded, then wished I hadn't because it hurt. But I didn't wince. The last thing I wanted was to be stuck here any longer. I had to get out of here. I had to find the jewelry before Sylvia acted out the rage I knew she must be feeling.

I did not relish joining the vampire knitting club.

Knowing Sylvia, she wouldn't even turn me into a vampire. She'd do something even worse.

No, I definitely needed to find those jewels.

CHAPTER 8

*R*afe helped me to the car and even put my seatbelt on for me. Gran said she was needed at home, and I guessed her mission would be trying to contain Sylvia. I didn't envy her that task.

I closed my eyes and leaned back as he drove the smooth, quiet car from the hospital. After a while, I opened them. Shouldn't I be home by now? And then I saw the canopy of trees linking overhead, the moon and stars far above and realized we weren't heading back to my flat. He was taking me to his manor house.

I thought about arguing, but really, settling into that soft bed, knowing that William, Rafe's efficient butler and excellent cook, was there to look after me was wonderful. Even better, if Sylvia wanted to get to me, she would have to go past Rafe. She might be furious, and I knew she would be, but I would back Rafe against any force, alive or undead.

"Is Sylvia very angry?" I asked Rafe as we pulled up to his manor house.

There was a tiny pause, and I could feel his cold anger

without him saying a word. "Leave Sylvia to me," he said curtly.

Oh, boy, she must be really mad.

And she was right to be. I put my hand to my aching head. "I can't believe I was so stupid. He seemed so inoffensive, that little man. The accountant. He asked me to meet him in a quiet room. Away from the crowd, away from the security, away from everybody. What was I thinking?"

He glanced over at me but didn't say anything.

I answered his unasked question anyway. "He said he had concerns. Something about the production was bothering him and he didn't want to talk about it in front of everybody." I rubbed my head. "What a patsy. That must be the oldest trick in the book. So, like a fool, I went to meet him."

"And then what happened?" Rafe asked in a quiet, not at all accusing tone. That made it easier for me to remember.

"He wasn't there."

"Try and remember exactly what happened. Everything you remember. A sound, a sight, a smell."

"I remember being hit over the head." Well, that wasn't exactly true. I remembered the terrible burst of pain and then that sense of falling. I didn't even remember hitting the ground.

"I felt something or someone behind me. I went to turn my head, and that's when he hit me."

"I should have been there." He sounded furious, and I realized it wasn't with me but himself. "It was dangerous for you to go there with a fortune in uninsured jewels hanging off you. It was so wrong of Sylvia to treat you like a mannequin. We all should have known better."

I appreciated his support, but how could any of us have

known? It had seemed perfectly safe. And it would have been if I hadn't slipped away from the crowd to meet with someone I didn't even know.

I knew that if they had any ideas where the jewels were, he'd have told me by now, but still, I had to ask.

"Are there any clues?"

"None. Your accountant seems to have made a clean getaway."

"I will find him," I said. "I don't want to say if it's the last thing I do, because with Sylvia around, it might well be. But what's he going to do with them? It's not like he pilfered something from a regular jeweler. Something mass-produced that you could sell on eBay."

"No. Sylvia says any jeweler or collector will recognize the set immediately."

"You've spoken to Sylvia?" My voice came out really eager and desperate.

"I have."

"Does she have any ideas?"

"She does not."

"I have to call her."

"I wouldn't advise it. At least, not until she calms down."

It was gratifying to see that the minute we pulled up, the big doors to the mansion opened and William came hurrying out. He opened my door even before Rafe could do it, and between them, they helped me out. I laughed and then wished I hadn't because it hurt so much.

"I can walk, you know."

William looked at both of us. "Oh, let Rafe do his He-Man thing. He's going to anyway."

And then I found myself picked up once again and held

against Rafe's chest. I was even more like Scarlett O'Hara now, being carried into that beautiful mansion. And up those stairs.

He took me into the room that was pretty much known as mine. Fortunately, I kept some extra clothes and underwear and toiletries here. I couldn't go around in an evening gown for much longer.

I rejected both their offers to help and got myself undressed and into my pajamas. It was nearly three in the morning. In the en suite bathroom, I inspected myself and found that my face looked pale and drawn.

I washed my face and brushed my teeth and then crawled into the big bed.

William came in with a tray. It was as though he'd read my mind. "It's a little soup and some chamomile tea. I thought that might help calm you."

"You're a saint."

He left and then Rafe came in and sat on the edge of the bed.

"You're not to worry about anything. Get a good night's sleep."

"But the police?"

"They'll be here in the morning," he said soothingly.

I wanted to argue, but I didn't have the strength. When I was done, he took the tray from me and then pulled the quilt up over my shoulders.

Then he leaned forward and kissed my aching head. "Things will look brighter in the morning," he said. "I promise."

Amazingly, I slept the night through. I didn't wake up until after nine the next morning, and I was feeling a lot more human. My head still ached, but a couple of painkillers took it down from acute to manageable. My vision wasn't blurry. I could remember pretty much everything, including the fact that one of the most powerful and scary vampires in the world was no doubt my sworn enemy right now, and while my headache was still present, it seemed to me in keeping with a bash on the head yesterday.

I showered carefully and left my hair to do its own thing. The thought of a comb or blow-dryer or a brush was too much. I dressed in comfy sweats and padded downstairs. I found William in the kitchen, where he'd obviously been waiting for me. He looked at me searchingly before he spoke.

"How are you feeling?"

"I've been better," I told him.

He came forward, and I could see him searching my eyes to see if they looked okay. He was so sweet. "Coffee's on, and breakfast is whatever you desire."

Truth to tell, I didn't have a great appetite. Which was a tragedy when I was in William's kitchen. I told him I'd start with the coffee, and then he tempted me with yogurt and fresh fruit and granola.

Rafe came in and was much less subtle than William. He tilted my chin and told me to open my eyes wide. The doctor had sent us home with a list of warning signs, and Rafe now asked things like whether I had weakness or dizziness. He made me walk up and down the kitchen and checked my gait and balance. He also seemed satisfied by what he saw, however.

I said, "I need to get back into town."

He shook his head. "Violet's running the shop. She's perfectly capable."

"It's not Violet I'm worried about. I need to talk to Sylvia."

He and William shared a glance. "Let Sylvia cool down. It wouldn't be a good idea for you to go near her right now."

"At least I should apologize. I never meant to—"

"Please, Lucy, trust me. She needs time to cool down."

No doubt he was right. "Well, then, I need to get to the college. And the police will want to talk to me."

Again they exchanged a glance. "The police are on their way here."

My eyes widened. "They are?"

"They need to talk to you about the theft."

Rafe sent me a warning glance. "Don't forget, Lucy, as far as the world knows, those jewels belong to you. Do we need to refresh your memory on how you came to be Sylvia's heir?"

"No. If there's one thing Sylvia was very good at, it was rehearsing me for my part. I'll be fine."

I finished my breakfast, brushed my teeth and tried to tidy my hair, but it was so hopeless, I gave up. I went back down and didn't know what to do with myself. I wandered around picking things up and putting them down. I picked up one of the books that Rafe stocked, but in truth, I couldn't concentrate. Finally, I slipped on a sweater and went out into the garden.

Henri, a resident peacock who was more like a pampered pet, came waddling up. The peacock is one of the most beautiful birds on earth, but Henri was not a tip-top specimen. His feathers were bedraggled, and he had to be borderline obese for a peacock. But what he lacked in beauty, he more than made up for in personality. Luckily, I might be concussed, but I wasn't stupid. I'd made William give me a few pieces of steak, Henri's favorite food, and the bird happily and gently took the pieces out of my hand.

Then I walked around. The morning was misty and made the grounds around Rafe's manor house look almost like a painting. My reverie wasn't a happy one. All I could think about was the night before. How Sylvia had entrusted me with her prized possessions and how I had let them be stolen.

The accountant had seemed so nervous and so sincere, I'd let him lure me to a quiet alcove. Honestly, if my head hadn't already hurt so much, I'd have slapped myself upside it. How could I have been so stupid?

I knew I had to stop beating myself up and instead turn my energy towards trying to figure out how to find the guy. As Rafe had said, these weren't the kind of jewels that you could easily fence. Maybe there was a chance we could get them back.

If not, I was pretty sure I was going to have to buy myself a ticket back to America. So long as Sylvia was living underneath the shop and I was living above it, I didn't think I'd sleep a wink.

Rafe's words floated across my mind. He'd told me that he wouldn't let Sylvia hurt me, and I knew he wouldn't. Still, I didn't want to go through life safe only because I had a big, strong protector. Not that I minded having a big, strong protector. I was glad and flattered. But at some point, I needed to stand on my own two feet.

That meant I had to find those jewels.

While I was walking, Henri trailing my steps hopefully, William came out.

"Lucy, the police are here."

I took a quick breath in.

I turned to Henri. "And it's showtime."

Henri put his head to one side and regarded me from his beady, bright eyes. He had no interest in showtime. He only cared about mealtime.

Disgusted at the lack of steak being offered, he turned and waddled away.

And I went back into the manor house to face the police.

CHAPTER 9

I was interviewed by a sergeant who asked the obvious questions. Had I noticed anyone suspicious at the gala? No.

Had anyone paid particular attention to the expensive jewels I was wearing? Yes. Everyone.

Were they insured? No.

Did I have any idea who might have taken them? No.

The interview went on for about ten minutes more, but the trouble was I didn't have anything helpful to offer, and I suspected the interview was part of a checklist of action items that would end up in a file somewhere.

I stayed at Rafe's for two days and then decided to go back to work. I opened my shop and was aware of a feeling of nervousness in the pit of my stomach. I couldn't help but keep thinking of the vampires who lived just beneath my feet. And of one vampire in particular, who definitely had me on her hit list. I didn't want to anger a vampire at the best of times, but Sylvia? I'd have gone very far out of my way not to have her as an enemy.

I got through the day somehow, but I could almost feel the anger and resentment floating up from their subterranean nest.

I waited until ten o'clock that night, pacing up and down miserably in my flat. Then I couldn't stand it anymore. I had to talk to her. Rafe had warned me to give her time and space, but I couldn't do it. I was a nervous wreck.

I went downstairs, and the darkened shop seemed creepy and unfriendly for almost the first time I could remember. I walked through the back where I ran the knitting club, and the empty chairs sat in the darkened room like so many fingers wagging at me in disapproval.

I almost turned tail when I got to the trapdoor. But I made myself continue. I lifted it and went down the rough-hewn stairs into the tunnels. I never liked coming down here, even when I was not alone. But for what I was about to do? I really had to steel myself. I heard a rustling somewhere and assumed it was a rat. I hoped it was only a rat.

I made my way as quickly as I could to the inset door that led to the vampires' lair. I had to go against every instinct for self-preservation, which was screaming at me to turn around and run.

I took a deep breath and then I knocked on the door.

No going back now, I told myself.

It wasn't long before the door was opened and my grandmother was standing there. Normally she looked so pleased to see me. I expected her face to break out in a beaming smile and for her to pull me into a hug. But this time she looked unhappy to see me. Frightened even. Instead of inviting me in, she stepped out and pulled the door to behind her.

"Lucy," she whispered. "What are you doing here?"

"I have to see her. I have to explain."

She glanced behind her and then back at me. "It's not a good idea."

Now I wasn't the only one pretty much telling me to turn tail and run. Maybe I should. Then a voice I both knew and dreaded called out from behind Gran.

"Is that her?"

Oh, great, I didn't even get the courtesy of her using my name. I was now *her*. Sylvia's tone was not welcoming.

I could see Gran wracking her brain, but what was she going to say? A pizza delivery guy had accidently knocked on a door that was almost impossible to find if you didn't know it was there? While she dithered, I pulled my courage together one more time and stepped past Gran and into the vampires' lair.

"Sylvia," I said. "I want to talk to you."

Every line of her body vibrated fury and loathing as she looked at me. No. Not at me. She was too angry to look me in the face. Her gaze went over my head as though I were literally beneath her notice. "And what could you possibly have to say for yourself?"

I had to remember she'd been an actress in the silent movie days, so she was used to emoting. But man, that woman could emote. Her eyes were glacial. And her face seemed to be set in stone.

I had to swallow before I could even speak. "I'm sorry. That's all I wanted to say to you. I'm so sorry."

I thought her head might explode. "Sorry?" she shrieked. "I put into your possession a priceless set of jewels. All you had to do was hang onto them for a couple of hours in a crowded room, with security. How on earth did you manage to mess it up? A task so simple Mabel could have managed it."

"No need to insult me," Mabel said from behind her.

"Honestly, I don't know what happened." My voice came out wimpy and shaky. I felt Gran come up beside me, a silent, guarding presence.

She said, "It took a lot of courage for her to come here, Sylvia."

Sylvia struck a pose and looked up at the ceiling. "Boring," she said in a single, cold word, stretching it out so that I could feel the icicles prick me.

Gran was right. It had taken every ounce of courage I possessed, and I didn't have much left in stock. I said, "Well, I really am sorry. I never meant for this to happen. I'm doing everything I can to try and find them."

Now she skewered me again with her cold gaze. "Everything? What are you doing here then?" She leaned forward, right into my face, and I took a step backwards. "Everything? Everything is spending every moment of your time talking to everyone who was there. Making the police put more manpower behind this. Don't come here with some whiny, pathetic, little 'I'm sorry.' Show me you are sorry by finding my jewels."

"That's easier said than done. How am I supposed to make the police make this more of a priority? They're treating the attack on me as an assault," and I didn't tell her that that was the part they were much more concerned about than the theft of a few jewels. "It's not like it was a murder."

She looked at me, and I could read her gaze as though she'd spoken. If I had been killed, then the police would take it more seriously.

Theodore came out of his room looking very dapper and obviously ready to go out for the evening. He looked surprised to see me there. "Lucy. How are you feeling?"

I was so grateful to him. He was the only person who'd asked me how I was after being horribly attacked.

I turned away from Sylvia and said, "I still have a headache, but I'm feeling much better. Thank you for asking."

"You should be upstairs resting," he said kindly.

"Resting?" Sylvia shrieked again. Then she poked at me with a long, bony finger. "You do not rest. Not for an instant until you've found my jewels."

Theodore looked at her. "Has it occurred to you, Sylvia, that instead of these histrionics, you might also help Lucy find the jewels?"

"Me? What's it to do with me?"

Theodore was a good private investigator. And he thought like one. He looked from her to me and back again. "I've been wondering why."

"Why what?"

"Why did this production company come to you for your jewels?"

She looked puzzled by the question. I felt puzzled too, but I had an inkling of where he was going with this.

"Who else would they go to?" she asked. She was so taken up with her anger and bitterness and grief over her loss that she was having trouble thinking clearly. Maybe there was no more room in her head.

Theodore said, "Think about it. It's one thing to make a movie, but what was the process by which you were somehow approached about those jewels? You've been out of

77

the public eye for some time. And so have the Cartier jewels. Who even knew you had them?"

For the first time, I saw her fury begin to abate a bit as she started to think. Her eyes narrowed on Theodore's face. "What are you saying?"

"I'm wondering if the theft wasn't a sudden, random event. But there was more planning behind it."

"Nonsense. Of course, once the producers did their research, they were going to find out about the jewels. I was very famous. So were the Cartier brothers. Jacques was my particular friend. Put us together, and you had something priceless and irreplaceable."

The way she said priceless and irreplaceable and stared at me while saying it was like being poked through the heart. Twice.

Theodore seemed impervious to the stabbing. Mostly because it wasn't happening to him. He said, "Who first approached you?"

She shrugged her elegant shoulders as if it was beneath her notice to worry about that kind of thing. "My lawyer. I didn't care about the details."

"Could you find out?"

She heaved a great sigh as though this was all a terrible inconvenience. "I'm sure you're wrong."

"Then that's an avenue of inquiry that I can close off," he said in his gentle way. "That's what an investigation is, you know. I follow leads and make guesses and talk to people, and as I get answers, the path narrows. In the end, I do get there."

"You mean you'll find my jewels?"

"You know we're all trying our best, Sylvia. It's time for you to put away your rage and start actively helping."

I took another step back. I couldn't believe he'd been so bold as to say such a thing to the furious actress. But, to my surprise, instead of flying at him, she took a deep breath. "Nothing will make me give up my rage until those jewels are found. However, I will ask my lawyer who approached him and when."

"And I have some contacts in the underworld. I'll see if anyone's tried to fence the jewels."

Gran said, "They're so recognizable. Isn't it likely they'll have been broken up?"

The minute she finished speaking, I could tell Gran wished she could swallow her tongue. I wish she'd thought it through too before she'd said those words. We must all have been thinking it, except for poor Sylvia. I really didn't think that possibility had occurred to her. She turned to stare at Gran.

"Broken up?"

Gran scrambled to backpedal. "I'm sure they haven't been. It's such a marvelous set. Of course, anyone would want to keep it as is. I don't know what I was thinking. I'm a foolish, old woman. Don't listen to me."

But, of course, that was the most likely thing that had happened to the jewels. Theodore stepped in again. "Let's not jump to any conclusions. I'll find out everything I can. Try not to worry."

CHAPTER 10

*P*atricia Beeton walked into Cardinal Woolsey's Knitting and Yarn Shop the next morning with a worried frown on her face. She looked much less glamorous now that she was wearing regular person clothes: jeans and a chunky, green sweater with a multicolored scarf. She carried a large bag.

"Lucy," she said, "how are you feeling? I wouldn't have had such a thing happen for the world." A shudder went through me just looking at Patricia Beeton and recalling that pleasant chat we'd had while Sylvia's priceless jewels were still hanging around my neck, earrings, wrists and finger.

"My head still aches a bit, but the worst of it is losing that priceless set of jewels."

She hesitated. "I wasn't sure whether this was the right thing to do, but I've got that photograph I promised you." From her bag she pulled a photographer's folder, and inside it was an eight by ten glossy of the two of us standing at the gala.

We were leaning into each other, laughing. If it hadn't

all gone so terribly wrong, I'd have loved to have this photograph and loved to show it to Sylvia. As it was, it made my stomach clench. I summoned a wan smile and thanked her. She looked at me with worry in her eyes. "Lucy, I wouldn't have had this happen for the world. No one would. I keep wracking my brains to think—was there someone who was there that shouldn't have been? But of course, they'd hired actors to dispense the drink and food and so on. Any one of them could have been light-fingered."

I knew all this. "Are they having any luck tracking all those people down?"

She made a face. "The agency's doing its best. But nothing so far. I suspect quite a few of them would prefer not to chat with the police. Well, they're indigent actors. Most of them have something in their past. They've gone bankrupt, defaulted on student loans, a bit of drug possession and some unruly conduct." She shrugged. "They're actors."

We chatted for a few moments more, and then it got awkward. She said brightly that she was going to start work on a new knitting project. She looked up and there, on the back wall, were hanging those beautiful, diamond-stitch sweaters that Gran and Hester had made. She let out a cry of delight. "Perfect. I was wondering what to make my family for Christmas. I can do one of those in each color."

Since she had four people on her close gift-giving list, I busied myself pulling together the wools for her.

While I did, I wondered if part of the reason she suddenly had all this knitting time was because the theft had caused problems for the movie's schedule. With all those journalists there, the gala had definitely made the news, with the focus ending up not on the exciting new production of an old classic but on the jewel heist.

"Has it affected your contract?" I asked her, counting out the blue wool.

"What? The attack at the gala? I don't know. I never had a signed contract."

I stared at her and promptly lost count. "You didn't have a signed contract?"

"No. Annabel had called me about the project and we discussed details, but I wasn't officially hired yet."

"Is that normal?"

She gave a brief laugh. "What's normal in the entertainment business?" Then she grew serious. "Annabel promised me the job, so I didn't worry about it."

"And now?"

She shrugged. "I haven't heard from her. But I think she's got other things on her mind."

I'd fetched wool for three sweaters, but I was short on the red. "It's been the most popular. But I've got more of the red wool on back order. It should be here in a few days."

"I'll have plenty to keep me busy. Let me know when it's in. You've got my mobile number? It's the best way to reach me."

I pulled up her file on the computer and double-checked I had her number.

She went away with a much more sizable bag than she'd arrived with and more sincere but not very helpful promises to do everything she could to help find Sylvia's jewels.

I left the folder on the counter. Normally I'd have pinned it up on my community board, where I liked to showcase my customer's creations. But I wouldn't be able to come into the store every day if I had to look at that first thing. If—no, when the jewels were found, I'd hang that picture up in pride of place.

She'd barely gone when Gran and Sylvia came out of the back room. No doubt they'd come up through the trapdoor and were planning to go out the front of my shop, but one of the features of the vampire is exquisitely keen hearing. There was no doubt they'd heard every word.

Sylvia's face was a combination of ice and fury. Not an attractive look on anyone. And a very dangerous one on a powerful vampire. She stalked towards me, and instinctively, I took a step back. But she didn't reach for me. She reached for the photograph folder still sitting innocently on my desk. I wanted to stop her, but my mouth was too dry to speak. For one agonizingly long minute, she stared at the photograph. Gran, looking nervous, peered over her shoulder and said in a falsely bright tone, "You'll get them back, my dear. I know you will."

In answer, Sylvia picked up the photograph and tore it in two pieces. The sound of the tearing paper felt like something sharp scratching its way down my spine.

She glared at me coldly, dropped the pieces onto the counter, turned on her heel and stalked towards the door.

Gran looked up at me nervously. "Try not to worry, love. I'm sure we'll find them. I'm sure we will."

I knew one thing. If we didn't, I was going to have to find a new place to live. And it was going to be as far away from Oxford as was geographically possible.

When the door shut behind them, I picked up the two pieces of the picture. Sylvia had managed to tear it so that both me and her jewels were torn in half. Perhaps the message was only one of anger, but to me it felt like a threat. I was about to throw the thing in the garbage when something caught my eye.

In the background, behind where we'd been standing, were two people in an intense conversation. It wouldn't have been noticeable when the picture was whole because the photographer was so good. The jewelry was so spectacular and our smiles so bright that the eye was automatically drawn there. But with the thing torn in two, the background became more visible. Bryce Teddington was in deep conversation with a pale young woman I'd never seen before.

I wondered who she could be. I remembered how intense he'd been with me. What had he been talking about with that young woman so shortly before disaster befell us all? Could she have been an accomplice?

If we could find the mystery woman, might we find Bryce Teddington and Sylvia's jewels?

I contacted Theodore immediately, and I think I got him out of bed, but he promised he'd be with me as quickly as possible. I stared a minute longer at that picture and then called Rafe and told him what I'd found.

I debated with myself, then told him about the incident with Sylvia. "She ripped me in half. Do I need to be worried? You know that expression, if looks could kill? Every time Sylvia looks at me, my blood gets a bit colder."

In a low, furious undertone, he said, "If she touches so much as a hair on your head…" The menace seemed even deeper when he didn't finish the sentence. I began to think I might not be in as much danger as the glamorous vampire.

Before I could even tell him about the photograph, he said, "I'm coming over."

He must have already been in Oxford doing business, for he arrived at the shop in about ten minutes. I'd never been so glad to see anyone. I had to remember that as much as they were my friends, and as good to me as Sylvia had been, a vampire didn't have to play by the same rules as mortals. If she completely lost her head and took my life, what repercussions would there be?

Rafe would probably make an end of her. And my poor gran would then lose both her granddaughter and her best friend. I couldn't let that happen. The only way to get Sylvia back to looking at me without hatred and bloodlust in her eyes was to find those diamonds. And fast. That or I was seriously going to have to leave Oxford. As much as I'd come to love it here, and as much as I loved my gran and had strong, if complicated feelings for Rafe, I couldn't continue. Not like this.

Rafe arrived, and the cheerful tinkle of the bells on the door was at odds with the cold, hard expression on his face. "Where is she?"

"She's out," I said, having no doubt at all who he was referring to.

He made a sound far too much like a growl for my comfort. He said, "You are not going to be in this store alone. Not while she's a danger."

I'd already thought of that. "I can get Polly and Scarlett to help in the shop when Violet's not available."

He shook his head sharply. "Not mortals. And not a self-involved witch. The only ones who are strong enough to stop Sylvia are her own kind."

I looked at him. "Who are you suggesting? Mabel and Clara?"

"Don't discount them. They're more powerful than they look."

"As powerful as Sylvia?"

He tapped his fingers on the countertop. "Probably not. Better that you don't come into the shop at all. Let your lazy cousin do some work for a change. She should earn that generous salary you pay her."

Since he had no idea how much I paid Violet, I knew he was just letting off steam. "You're coming back with me. Go pack a bag."

"Rafe..." I didn't get any further. He reached out and grabbed my hand. His eyes bored into mine and I saw, not for the first time, how much he cared.

"If anything happened to you..." He didn't have to finish the sentence. I knew one thing. While I was in Rafe's care, I'd be completely safe.

But I wasn't a shrinking violet. I didn't want to be pampered and kept in cotton wool. I'd go crazy. So I leveled my own tough-guy stare at him. Well, as much as I could do a tough-guy stare, which wasn't anything to be proud of. "One condition. We do everything we can to find these jewels. And you do not shut me out. Otherwise I'll stay here and take my chances."

A shaft of humor lightened those wintry eyes a little. "You with your bargains. Always so American."

That was his way of saying yes.

Rafe went to the door and turned the open sign to closed. My heart rate bumped up. "What are you doing?"

He walked back. "This isn't where I intended to have this conversation, but there is a little matter of a marriage proposal before you."

My pulse went all fluttery. "Rafe, this isn't exactly the best time."

"Marry me. At least then I'd have you under my roof. I could keep you safe."

I felt so wretchedly indecisive. It wasn't that I hadn't been thinking about his proposal. When I wasn't sick with dread about Sylvia's missing jewels, I thought of little else. "But you would lose me. I will age as a normal, human woman. I'll get old and wrinkly and sag."

His eyes lit with humor at that. "I don't care."

I knew he didn't. He'd been through it once before with his first wife. But that had been half a millennium ago. "Rafe. It took you five hundred years to get over the last mortal woman you loved. Are you sure you want to do this again?"

His hand tightened on my wrist. "As sure as I've ever been of anything. I think my track record proves that I am nothing if not a faithful husband."

I couldn't argue with that. I felt foolish and indecisive, but it was a big decision. Marriage in general was a big decision. And I'd never had the best taste in men. Oh, I knew I could trust him. I knew he loved me. I even knew that I loved him. But I'd age, and he wouldn't. How long would it be before people were looking at me like I was the ultimate cougar? At some point, we'd have to leave Oxford. At some later point, I would no doubt have to pretend to be his old aunt or his mother or something, while he remained forever thirty-five and in his prime. While I aged and aged and grew more and more frail and finally died. I didn't want that for him. I didn't want it for me. Of course, another alternative was before me. I supposed I could always join him. Have him turn me into a vampire. But I didn't want to make that choice. Constance, his first wife, hadn't chosen it, either.

I looked at him. My answer trembled on my lips and then a cheerful voice said, "So you found a clue? Well done, Lucy." And Theodore walked in from the back room.

CHAPTER 11

*R*afe released my wrist. He turned to Theodore. "For a detective, you have a wretched sense of timing."

Or perhaps an impeccable sense of timing. I knew I would have to give Rafe an answer, but at least I didn't have to give it right now.

I took a moment to pull myself together, and then I picked up the torn halves of the photograph and put them on the counter before the two vampires. Rafe's hand clenched immediately into a fist as he looked down at the image of me torn in half. "Did she do this?"

I didn't answer. He knew perfectly well who had done it.

Theodore said in a calm, soothing tone, "Do you have some tape, Lucy?"

I was grateful for his matter-of-fact handling of this awkward moment. I nodded and fussed around in a drawer where I kept everything from spare pens to stray elastic bands and scissors and stamps and envelopes and there, right at the back, was the tape. I pulled it out and said, before I even handed it to him, "What I noticed was this," and I pointed to what would have been the background of the picture. "That's Bryce Teddington." I pointed to the other person. "And that does not look like a casual conversation."

Theodore pulled a magnifying glass from his pocket. He looked like a cherub-faced, chubby Sherlock Holmes as he studied the pair. "Do you know who it is, Lucy?"

"No idea. But I think it might be worth finding out. That is not cocktail party chit-chat those two are having."

"No." He peered closer. "And look at that."

I peered through the enlarging lens and saw what he'd meant. There was a piece of paper, and one of them was handing it to the other. It was impossible to tell in that captured moment whether the unknown person was giving the paper to Bryce Teddington or Bryce Teddington was giving the paper to the other person. Either way, I suspected the unknown woman was going to be a person of interest in this case.

"I have an idea," I said. I put my camera on maximum magnification and then took a photograph of the two people in the picture. Fortunately, that professional photographer had been good enough that the people in the background were still recognizable. Then I texted the image to Patricia Beeton and asked her if she knew who the person was.

Instead of texting me back, she phoned me. I was excited when I saw who was calling, hoping she could tell me who the mysterious woman was. But what she said was, "I remember that woman. I was surprised she was at the party because she wasn't with the production company. She obviously wasn't one of the waitresses."

"Could she have been Bryce Teddington's date?" They had clearly been speaking intimately.

"No. We weren't allowed to take dates. Well, only Lord Pevensy, obviously, could take his wife. But it was confined to key staff at the production company, as many entertainment journalists as we could get and important people in the film business. There were some people who worked for the college there, though."

"Thanks, Patricia. You've been a great help."

"Anything I can do. We all feel terrible about this."

"I can imagine. I guess it's put a real hiccup in the production." Though they did say that there was no such thing as bad publicity. The notoriety of the theft of these famous jewels would probably increase ticket sales.

She made a strange sound. Something between a laugh and a groan. "The real question is whether this movie will be made at all."

I felt my eyes widen. "What?"

If we'd gone through all this and lost Sylvia's jewels and she didn't even get her movie remade? I might as well just buy myself a ticket to Antarctica right now.

"Annabel phoned me half an hour ago. She said Simon Dent is having second thoughts. He's very superstitious, it turns out, and thinks the jewel theft is a bad omen. Annabel's worried he doesn't want to be involved with Rune Films since their accountant seems to have stolen the Cartier set. She said the police came to their office and interviewed everyone who'd been at the gala. And they searched Bryce Teddington's office."

"Have they interviewed you?"

"No, but we were all searched before we could leave, you

know. And they asked every one of us if we'd noticed anything suspicious. I certainly didn't. I was having a nice time until I saw you being taken away by ambulance."

"Not a great end to the evening," I agreed. We ended the call. I wouldn't have thought this day could get any worse.

As so many times when I thought a day couldn't get worse, I'd been wrong.

I relayed the information to Rafe and Theodore. Then, I looked at that photograph again, pulling it right up close to my face and really studying the faces through that magnifying glass. And it was like Bryce Teddington was before me again. I replayed in my head that intense conversation we'd had. "I can't believe he stole the jewels. He seemed so nice. And so mild-mannered. I thought he was trying to warn me of something."

"Which is how he lured you away from the main room into a quiet alcove where he could hit you over the head without anyone being any the wiser," Rafe said in an unnecessarily sarcastic tone.

I winced inside. He was right, of course. I'd been so gullible.

"Well, Patricia Beeton knows everybody at the production company. She didn't recognize that woman. She thinks she works for the college."

Rafe and Theodore looked at each other and then at me. "Then I guess we'd better get ourselves to the college."

"But what about my shop? I can't leave it. It's three o'clock in the afternoon. It's bad enough you put the closed sign up. What if I actually had customers?"

Rafe turned to Theodore. "Go wake up Mabel, will you? Or Clara. Either of them would be only too pleased to spend a couple of hours in the shop. You know they're always dying to work behind the counter, Lucy."

It was true. I still hesitated. Not because they were undead so much as their terrible taste. Especially Mabel. But I couldn't worry about that now. I'd have no shop at all if I didn't find Sylvia's jewels again.

Rafe made a call to the college, while Theodore went down to rouse one of the vampire knitters.

Within a very short period of time, both Mabel and Clara showed up. They looked a little sleepy but quite pleased with themselves. Mabel was wearing the garment she'd begun the other night. It looked like she was wearing a bath mat with sleeves.

I told them I'd only be a couple of hours and thanked them sincerely for their help.

"Oh, it's a pleasure, dear. And if you're not back by five, we can manage to close the shop."

I nodded, truly grateful to them, keeping my eyes averted from the bath mat sweater. And then the three of us left.

We purred through the streets in Rafe's black Tesla. We could have walked to the college in about twenty minutes, but it was undeniably quicker this way.

St. Peter's was one of the oldest and most famous colleges in all of Oxford. Built in 1200 over the ruins of a former college, it had appeared in movies and television shows galore, including a few exterior scenes from the original *The Professor's Wife,* which was why we'd ended up having the gala there.

When I recalled how thrilled I'd been the last time I was on the campus, my feelings could not have been more different than they were now. Then I'd been wearing a priceless set of jewels, doing a big favor to a vampire I really cared about, being photographed as though I were an A-list movie star. Now I was slinking along with a weight of guilt on me much heavier than the weight of those jewels had been.

We walked in the front door, and I couldn't help but remember how fabulous it had been when I walked up on the red carpet and everything had seemed so bright and exciting. Now I slunk in like a student with failing grades. As though Rafe could read my thoughts, he put an arm around my shoulders and leaned in.

"It's not your fault. We all know that Sylvia pushed you into showing off her Cartier set. The responsibility is hers, and when she calms down, she will realize it."

"Thanks," I said softly.

Rafe was the kind of guy that when he made a phone call, people jumped. He was a well-respected expert in antiquarian books and manuscripts, but he was also really well connected. We were met by a portly man in tweeds who obviously knew Rafe.

Rafe introduced him as Piers Gimlet, head of security. He shook his head. "Terrible thing. Of course, it's the worst possible publicity for us. We've had parents on the phone worrying that it's not safe to send their children here."

So not what I was worried about right now. We headed in and Rafe showed him the picture and asked him if he knew the young woman who was standing beside Bryce Teddington. He studied the photograph carefully and I grew hopeful until he shook his head.

"I don't know everyone at the college, of course, but I've never seen this woman."

I noticed a tour group walking by and overheard the tour

guide, who looked to be a senior student, encouraging them to look up at the Jacobean ceiling. The group was staring up in rapt astonishment.

"Will ya look at that, Jackie?" a guy said in a New Jersey accent. I'd become so used to listening to the clipped, British accent that I felt drawn to this guy who made his enthusiasm known in a loud voice. He was short and squat and bald, and a big camera rested on his paunch.

"Now, if you'd come this way, I'll take you into the main floor gallery."

I don't know what instinct compelled me, but while Rafe and Theodore were in close conversation with Piers Gimlet, I slipped among the tour group. I wanted to go back into that room where the gala had occurred and look at it again with fresh eyes, and not under the scrutiny of their head of security. The young tour guide went on enthusiastically about the famous people who had studied there and some of the college traditions. And then, with a twinkle in his eye, he said, "I probably shouldn't tell you this, because it will be very shocking, but this room holds a great secret."

I bet this guy took part in amateur theatricals. He'd spoken the words with such drama that everybody, even my friend from New Jersey, hung on his every word. He said, "In previous times, of course women were not allowed in the college. This space was often used for smaller dinners. The gentlemen would sit back with their port and discuss the matters of the day. It was considered in very poor form to leave the room for any reason." He gave a humorous look at all of us and continued, "After drinking a vast quantity of port, you can imagine that sometimes nature's call was quite persistent. And to this end, there is a secret doorway." He gestured with his hand and low down in the wall. He leaned down, did something—maybe he only pulled the corner of what looked like stone—and a door swung open. "It's completely imperceptible if you didn't know that it was there," he said.

Everyone gathered around to peer inside. Inside it was a small cupboard containing a chamber pot. Laughter and whispers went around the group, but I just stared at the spot, my whole body tingling. And I waited for the rest of the story. "Having relieved himself, the diner would then place the full chamber pot back in the alcove and shut the door. On the other side of the alcove, a butler would open the opposite door, remove the brimming chamber pot, empty its contents and replace it with a clean one."

I couldn't even believe it. I turned and rushed out of the room. I went so fast that the tour guide said, "Miss? Are you feeling all right?"

I didn't even stop. I just threw one hand up and gave him half a wave.

I found Rafe and Theodore still in deep conversation with Piers Gimlet. They were obviously discussing what measures were being taken. I waited impatiently for a pause and said, "I think I know what they did with the jewels after they stole them."

That got everyone's attention. I looked at the three men. "Everyone was searched leaving the gala, right?"

"Yes. That's right," Piers Gimlet said. "Every guest and every staff member. There was some sharp grumbling, I can tell you, but they all complied."

"But what if the jewels weren't taken out of the college? At least not then."

Theodore narrowed his gaze on my face. "What are you getting at, Lucy?"

"There's a secret alcove in the gallery."

The head of security looked at me as though I was mad, and then I could see the moment that realization dawned. "That's a curiosity that we've kept for the tourists."

Rafe ignored him and stared at me. "What curiosity?"

I quickly reiterated the story of the chamber pot. "It makes perfect sense. That's what they must have done. They stole the jewels and slipped them into the cupboard. Then, while there was pandemonium in the main room and everyone's bags were searched on their way out, all Bryce Teddington had to do was go around the other side, open the other secret door, shove the jewels in his pocket and walk out a different exit."

Theodore shook his head. "Neither of you can ever tell Sylvia that her jewels were placed in a chamber pot."

CHAPTER 12

"*O*h, don't worry." Though at this point I thought she'd be so grateful to get them back, she wouldn't even care.

When we went back into the room, the tour group had moved on, and the head of security immediately went to the little cupboard. It was ingenious. He opened it, but of course the chamber pot was empty. However, it had opened so easily that I was convinced that's how the jewels had been hidden. "The black and white movie was playing on a screen right here," I told them. "It would have obscured the cupboard."

Theodore suggested we retrace my steps as much as we could. "You were wearing the jewels here," he said, standing in the middle of the room. I nodded. "And then Bryce Teddington convinced you to meet him."

I felt the weight of humiliation again as I realized what a fool I'd been. What a dupe. Still, I had to get over myself and try and help find the set. So I led the two of them down the hall exactly as I'd taken it.

"Did you see anyone?"

I tried to think back. Had I? I pointed to my left, to the ladies' room door. "A woman dressed like a flapper came out of the bathroom. I assumed she was a waitress, as they'd all dressed in period costume."

"Did she speak to you?"

"No."

"Did you recognize her? Had you seen her before?"

"There were a lot of people there. No. I didn't." They followed me down the hall, past the ladies'. I stopped again. "There was a full laundry cart there, but I think someone parked it there and left it."

We moved on to the alcove. I shuddered again, reliving the attack. Theodore listened as I described what happened. Then he looked around, backed up and gazed both ways. He said, "Bryce Teddington hit you over the head, stripped you of the jewels, and then walked back into the main room and deposited them in the secret alcove to be fetched later. That's what you're suggesting."

I looked at Rafe and then back to Theodore. "Maybe? Or he hit me over the head, and the woman in the photograph took the jewels and put them in the secret cupboard."

He didn't seem convinced. "Where does this corridor lead?" he asked Piers Gimlet.

"There's nothing down there but the laundries and then a door to the outside."

"May I?" Theodore asked. The man nodded, and we all followed. Sure enough, there were big, double doors leading to the laundry and then a door that went outside. Theodore paused and looked at the laundry but kept going. We followed all the way outside. It was chilly out there, and I wished I'd thought to bring a coat.

We were in a not very interesting quadrangle with grass and some trees and flowerbeds. The horticulture out here was a bit of an afterthought. All the glory was obviously focused on the front quadrangle.

A cool breeze suddenly kicked up, and I wrapped my arms around myself. Somewhere a door banged. A uniformed maintenance guy walked by. The head of security said to him, "There's a door banging somewhere."

"Aye. I'm going to investigate. If those students have broken the lock again on that ice house..." He sounded very annoyed.

Theodore perked up. "There's an ice house?"

The head of security said, "Yes. It's ancient. But it's always kept locked and bolted."

The uniformed security guy said, "Well, it's supposed to be. Until them ruddy kids get into it."

Theodore didn't ask permission this time. He just followed the maintenance guy. And then we all followed along. The ice house was nothing more exciting than a raised mound of grass until you got closer and saw there was a stairway leading down to a stout door. I could see where it was meant to be locked, but the lock was missing. If it hadn't been windy, it would have been impossible to tell. The guy went down to inspect the damage, Theodore right behind him. He muttered again, then opened the door to peer inside. Theodore eased his way around the man and went very still. Rafe and I followed and, even as Rafe tried to step in front of me and block my view, I peered around his shoulder.

I'd felt something dark coming from the other side of that door. I suspected he had too.

The ice house was an oval room about eight feet long and

probably as high. It was built of brick and definitely cooler than the air above. There was a scent of damp down here, and remains of old straw scattered on the floor. A mound of what looked like old laundry was pushed up against one side. The caretaker grumbled about kids as he stomped over to the bundled bedding. He reached down to it and pulled at the bundle. An arm flopped onto the ground at his feet.

"Come on, you, are you drunk?"

He knelt and pulled more bedding away.

I already had a bad feeling about this. The air felt heavy and dark to me. And the way Rafe had gone so still beside me, he knew too. There was more than a drunk student here.

Then the maintenance guy let out a cry and jumped back. "That bloke's not drunk. He's dead."

"Don't touch anything," Theodore ordered. The maintenance guy backed away, looking only too relieved not to have to figure out what to do. Theodore turned the body only long enough to reveal the face. With a cry of horror and sadness, I recognized Bryce Teddington.

CHAPTER 13

"Oh dear," Theodore said, looking down. "It's a homicide now."

Rafe looked at him. "Before the police arrive, let's make sure he doesn't have the jewels on him."

Theodore nodded, though I think we all knew it was doubtful indeed that Bryce Teddington would be lying dead in an obscure location and still have the jewels.

I couldn't look, so I backed out and listened as the maintenance guy filled in the head of security, who didn't look happy about this latest discovery. "We'll have to call the police. Again." And he glanced over at me as though this was my fault.

Rafe and Theodore came out, and Rafe shook his head at my inquiring gaze. No jewels, then.

"This changes everything," I said, thinking aloud.

Rafe nodded. "You're right. The theory that Bryce Teddington acted alone and escaped with the jewels is obviously not true. He must have had an accomplice. But I wonder who that was. And where they are now."

I pointed at Theodore, but what I was really pointing at was the torn photograph that he still had in his possession. If there was an accomplice, my money was on that girl he'd been having that intense conversation with only minutes before I was attacked.

He nodded. "It makes sense. It always seemed surprising to me that one man could knock you out, strip you of the jewels, and disappear so quickly. If he had an accomplice, that makes so much more sense."

I nodded. "They could have agreed to meet here later and share their haul. But what? They had an argument? She got greedy? And Bryce ended up dead."

Rafe took a moment to think. "Your theory doesn't hold, Lucy. Why meet here? Whoever had those jewels would have wanted to get off campus as quickly as possible." He looked down at the mound of earth, beneath which the poor man was lying there wrapped in sheets. The ice house had become his coffin.

"Remember, we passed the laundry." The wind lifted his black hair and ruffled it like affectionate fingers. "Didn't you say there was a cart full of laundry in the hallway?"

"Yes." I swallowed. "Are you saying...?"

He nodded. "I suspect someone had overheard your assignation. Bryce Teddington asked to meet you in an out-of-the-way location. Our murderer was already there when Bryce arrived. You've already told me that Bryce Teddington was an accountant and seemed like a very nervous individual. He would have got there first to make sure there was no chance of missing you. But the murderer was ahead of even him. The murderer took care of Bryce but, knowing you would be along shortly, couldn't take the time to dispose of him properly."

I was staring at him in growing horror. "You mean the killer threw Bryce in the laundry like a used towel?"

"I'm afraid so. In that cart of laundry you passed."

"Was he dead?"

"Impossible to say. Hopefully the police will be able to determine that."

"And then all they had to do was wait for me to show up, bash me over the back of the head and take the jewels."

I felt sick and shaky, and my head began to throb where I'd been hit so hard. "Maybe that's what he was telling that woman. That he was meeting me. But why didn't she kill me?"

"We don't know she's the killer. Let's not jump to more conclusions. Whoever attacked you may have intended to kill you, but there wasn't time."

My voice was slightly shaky as I said, "Because you showed up so fast."

"I told you. All you had to do was cry my name and I'd come to you."

"And did I?" I couldn't even remember. I recalled the terrible pain and the light flashing in front of my eyes and then darkness. Had I cried out Rafe's name on my way down?

"I heard you call me."

Okay, I could make excuses all I liked, but when I had been falling into darkness, for all I knew the last word I would ever speak had been his name.

THE MAINTENANCE GUY was left to stand guard over the ice house until the police arrived, and the rest of us went back inside the college.

The director of security called the police and, since we hadn't actually found the body, we thought it would be a good idea for us to leave. DI Chisholm and I had come across each other too often over dead bodies. And he and Rafe weren't exactly BFFs. I thought it was best for me, Rafe and Theodore to take a back seat on this one.

We got back into Rafe's car, and Theodore pulled out the torn photograph and studied it again. He shook his head. "I can't help the feeling that I know her from somewhere."

This was not surprising. The vampires had lived so long and come across so many people that they might see someone who looked vaguely like a person they'd known a couple of hundred years ago. Or, even if the acquaintance was more recent, there was a lot in the facial recognition database they had to sift through. Knowing this, I waited patiently. He squinted, got out the magnifying glass again. "I think her hair was different." The nice thing about a private investigator was he tended to be an observant man. "But I can't place her."

Seeing that she'd been seen at a function for a movie, I wondered if she was an actor who'd been hired as a server and chosen instead to conspire to steal jewels. "Maybe you've seen her on television or in the movies," I suggested.

"It's possible, I suppose. I must think about it. I'll get hold of the photographer. See what else he has. Maybe there are better shots of her."

I was very enthusiastic about this idea. "I hope the police do the same thing. I'm always reading about how the UK is so far ahead in facial recognition, and you can't go anywhere without being caught on CCTV. I bet they can find out who she is."

Theodore made a sound that was not exactly flattering towards British law enforcement. "All the fancy technology in the world doesn't replace good, old-fashioned policing," he informed me.

I gave him my biggest smile. "And you are the best."

That made him suddenly bashful. "Well, I don't say that. But dogged determination, you mark my words, Lucy, goes a long way."

He really was amazing at old-fashioned policing, but we had Hester and now Carlos, two young vampires who were extremely good with the computer. I thought that we pretty much had the tools of investigation, both modern and old-fashioned, nicely covered. If that woman was an actress of some sort, she shouldn't be that hard to find.

And when we did find her, I hoped the jewels were in her possession.

RAFE DROVE us back to Harrington Street, where Mabel and Clara had closed up for me. They'd done a wonderful job, which made me realize that I really could take a bit of time off if I needed to.

I collected Nyx, who was snoozing upstairs on the couch, but she was always ready to go anywhere with Rafe. Especially if he carried her draped over his shoulder.

I packed some essentials, and we decamped once more to Rafe's manor house, where William served a dinner of cioppino, thick Italian fish soup served with crusty bread. "I want your honest opinion, Lucy," he said when he served me. "I'm thinking of doing this as a main course for a small lunch I've been asked to cater."

I breathed in the scents of tomato, garlic, and a hint of fennel. There were big chunks of fish in there as well as prawns and mussels and clams still in their shells. "I'm already raving, and I haven't even tasted it yet," I said, picking up my spoon.

He stood beside me, waiting anxiously while I tasted and savored. I glanced up at him and grinned. "I hope you made a very large pot of this."

He put a hand on my shoulder. "I did."

Then he left the room, and Rafe sat watching me as I ate. It used to bother me, but I'd grown accustomed. Even as I dipped bread into the tasty broth, I was thinking hard. "Poor Bryce. Do you think he went quickly?" I hoped so.

"The forensics report will tell us a great deal." And, thanks to his connections, we'd have it as soon as the detectives. Possibly sooner. "I wouldn't feel too sorry for Mr. Teddington. The chances are good he was part of a plot to steal those jewels."

"I guess. But he seemed so nice."

William was as good as his word, and I'd barely finished my first bowl, with unbecoming haste, when he filled it again.

I ate this one more slowly, enjoying every bite and the wonderful bread William had baked fresh. After dinner, William brought me coffee in the lounge room, and we settled there. It was comfortable and, after the horror of finding Bryce Teddington dead, nice to feel safe. I'd have only brooded if I'd stayed in my flat. Even Nyx seemed happy to snooze at my side.

It wasn't long before Theodore showed up.

He'd successfully obtained the photographer's files from the gala evening. He brought them on a thumb drive, and the three of us sat in front of one of Rafe's big computers in his office. I was the only one who'd actually attended the gala, but they were looking for other things in the background, anything that seemed out of the ordinary or suspicious. Even better, I think we were all hoping that there'd be a glimpse of jewels passing from hand to hand or being secreted somewhere. It was a faint hope, but we were running pretty much completely on faint hope right now. The murder of Bryce Teddington took this from a probable crime of opportunity to something much more serious. Sure, the jewels were worth a heck of a lot of money, but I'd have taken a guess that Bryce Teddington thought his life was worth more. Besides, the penalty from theft to murder was a big jump in punishment by law. I felt awful now that I'd even blamed Bryce Teddington for their disappearance. I should have trusted my gut instincts. I thought he was a good guy. Neurotic and high-strung, but I had believed he could be trusted. It was an awful way to be proven right, to find his dead body. And, as Theodore reminded me, it didn't mean he hadn't been part of the conspiracy to rob me, only that once his part was played, he'd been cut out permanently.

Theodore also had the video footage. It was an odd experience to see myself not in a quick movie somebody had taken on their phone, or even those old movies on a camcorder that my mom used to embarrass me with when I was little, but to be filmed like I was a movie star. Watching myself on TV, I knew I'd never looked so glamorous in my whole life. And no doubt never would again. I saw myself getting out of the Bentley. I could almost see myself counting in my head that one and two and three moment of pause before I made my slow and stately way down the red carpet and into the college's main entrance. I looked so happy. A woman who has no idea that she's not stepping onto a red carpet; she's stepping into the worst minefield of her life. And one of those mines is about to blow up with her standing on it.

While we all watched the movie, I narrated it. "That's the executive producer, Peter. Then he takes me to Annabel, coming out to greet me. And then she's taking me to meet the executive producer, Lord Pevensy. He's the money man."

"Lord Pevensy," Rafe said. "I know him. And his wife."

Theodore said in a slightly dry tone, "I'm guessing she didn't marry him for his good looks."

"It's said that she spends his money faster than he can make it." Even in the video, you could see the carnal way the woman was staring at those jewels. I didn't want to jump to any conclusions or make threats against someone I knew little about, but Theodore was in the business of digging into ulterior motives. He said, "The Cartier collection would be a nice set of jewelry for anyone to have."

I told him how much she'd admired it, even reaching out to touch the diamonds at my throat, and the comments she'd made to her husband.

"Interesting," Theodore said, making a note in his ever-present notebook.

Rafe said, "But would she go to all that trouble for baubles she could never wear and would never be seen?"

He looked at me as though I'd have the answer, when I'd only met the woman for a few minutes. I had to agree with him though. She seemed like someone who'd want to wear her bling out, to be seen and envied.

Theodore said, "Still, it never hurts to check on people."

He was right. She might look like an ex-runway model, trophy wife, but for all we knew, she was really an international jewel thief. The longer I was alive, the more people surprised me.

The raw footage didn't last too much longer. And then we started to look at the still photographs. There were several hundred of them to get through, and we took our time with each one. I began to get sick of looking at my own face. Even more, I grew heartily sick of staring again and again at that necklace, the earrings sparkling from my lobes, the bracelets and the ring. The set seemed to have no other purpose than to remind me of how I had let Sylvia down.

I was sure she'd never forgive me. And I wasn't sure if I could ever forgive myself. If she'd been wearing them, she'd never have let herself be talked into going down a private hallway with a man she didn't know. I couldn't stop kicking myself for being such a fool.

Still, it was fascinating looking at those photographs. The people who were framed in the picture, the subjects, if you like, were smiling and laughing and posed together, but it was the people that didn't know they were being photographed who were so interesting to look at. Caught unawares, they displayed boredom. I was sure I saw looks of envy, and certainly more than one glance was cast at my neck area where the spectacular necklace sat, and what I saw was pure avarice.

I could imagine being an underpaid assistant of some sort invited along to this gala and then to see somebody who wasn't an A-list actress, but an ordinary woman who ran a knitting shop, elevated to star status and dripping with jewels that could not be insured because no one could place a value on them.

Sylvia had shown me a Christie's catalogue from some of Jacques Cartier's other early work, and the prices fetched were literally eye-popping. I mean, you could buy a small country for what people were willing to pay for a few shiny rocks. Okay, a few shiny rocks designed and turned into jewelry by some of the greatest talents in the 1920s. She'd collected catalogues over the years. Knowing Sylvia, she'd probably even been to some of the auctions, and she'd know the sale prices. Each time we came across one she'd say, "And of course, that was nothing near as nice as mine." Or, "Very inferior rubies." "Look at the inclusions on that diamond. One can see them with the naked eye." Maybe she could, with her vampire supervision, but to a mere mortal like me, they looked pretty swanky. And whoever had paid multimillions of Swiss francs, American dollars, Hong Kong dollars, euros, or British pounds had obviously felt the same way.

"Wait," I said, and before Theodore could move to the next photograph, I pointed in the upper left-hand corner. "That's Patricia Beeton, the clothing designer. And even though he's cut out of the frame, I'm certain she's talking to Bryce Teddington. I remember he was drinking sparkling water with lemon. And that looks like his watch. I only recognize it because he looked at it when we were picking a time to meet."

"Excellent work, Lucy."

"Theodore, let's see if we can find any other photo that shows the two of them together," Rafe said.

"Of course, it could be perfectly innocent. They could easily know each other. It's natural that they might exchange a few words," I said, not wanting to throw Patricia under a cloud of suspicion any more than I'd wanted to believe Bryce Teddington was capable of hitting me over the head and stealing my jewelry. I could be wrong in both cases, but I also wouldn't want Theodore to waste a lot of time following a trail that led to a blind alley.

Then I had an idea. "Patricia Beeton bought some woolen sweaters from me. I had to order in the extra wool. When it comes in, I'm to call her, and she'll come and pick it up."

"How long will that take?" Rafe asked me.

I bobbled my head back and forth. "Normally, three weeks. But if I found that wool in another store—"

Before I even finished the thought, Theodore was nodding. "I could drive up in the Bentley. I could have it to you within a day."

"Fabulous. And then, while we're chatting over wool, I'll casually get into a conversation about poor Bryce and how well did she know him."

"I'll prepare a list of questions for you. Things that you might not think to ask but that you could hopefully work into conversation naturally," Theodore said.

"And I'll make sure I'm close by," Rafe said. "As I believe I've told you many times before, Lucy, when you question someone who could be a murderer, you must expect danger."

CHAPTER 14

J nodded. Maybe at one time I'd believed he was overprotective, but I no longer did.

I yawned. I hadn't been sleeping well, for obvious reasons, and it was getting late. Rafe glanced up at me and then said to Theodore, "Let's go through the rest of these fairly quickly so Lucy can get to bed. After that, you and I will go through each frame and see if we can identify who else Bryce Teddington spoke to, Patricia Beeton spoke to, and the mysterious young woman who didn't seem to belong there at all."

We both agreed—Theodore because he normally did agree with Rafe, and me because I was dying to go to bed. Nothing too startling emerged as we went through the last fifty or so photographs, except that the young woman who had been seen in that first photograph talking to Bryce appeared several more times. Three times she was in the background talking to Bryce Teddington. In one frame, she appeared just behind Patricia Beeton's right shoulder. Had they just turned apart from an intense conversation? Or was it purely coincidence? She'd spoken to Lord Pevensy, and there was a photograph where Annabel was turning away from her with an irritated expression on her face. I wondered what that was about. Maybe she'd discovered the woman had no business there and was going to throw her out.

She didn't seem to be having a good time. I never saw her with a drink in her hand. In fact, her behavior was in every way suspicious. Twice Theodore said, "I wish I could place her. I know I've seen her somewhere."

I said, "We need somebody who watches a lot of TV who might recognize her."

They looked at each other and, as one, said, "Hester."

They agreed that Hester would be the next person to see the movie and the stills, but I warned them that they had to do it when Sylvia was nowhere to be found. "Better if Hester comes here. If Sylvia walked in and saw a movie of me wearing these jewels looking so glamorous... I'd rather talk to ten murderers than have to deal with the consequences."

I went to bed. I was so tired, I thought I'd drop right off to sleep, but my mind was racing. It was as though I was looking at those photographs all over again. Mostly I saw the jewels in all their very many poses, so clearly the star of the show.

Gran had tactlessly mentioned them being broken up, and I'd assumed that's what would happen to them too, but I thought back to Sylvia going to those auctions of pieces she had no intention of buying—well maybe she had, I don't know—pieces also by Cartier, her favorite jewelry designer. She'd kept the auction programs. Part of the reason she'd kept them was that she liked to collect her favorite designer.

I sat up in bed. What if the thief was a collector? What if it was one of those obsessed fans who had the kind of money that they could afford to buy something never seen outside their own walls?

I threw my clothes back on quickly and ran back to the office. Theodore and Rafe were still staring intently at the screen. And I thought in that moment that if anybody or any being could solve this puzzle, it would be them. They were completely focused and intent. And it wasn't just the thrill of the chase. I knew that they genuinely cared about Sylvia and wanted her to have her property back. Also, they genuinely cared about me and didn't want me to have my head ripped off or my throat ripped out or whatever Sylvia could do at her worst. I knew that they mostly stayed away from the old ways of feeding, but I hadn't forgotten that it was Sylvia who had turned my grandmother into a vampire. I knew she'd done it with the best of intentions, but that also meant that she was perfectly willing to fall back on the old ways if need be. I suspected, when consumed with rage, she might also do something she would later regret.

Naturally they heard me coming and both looked up inquiringly. I told them about Sylvia keeping all those programs, and immediately Theodore looked at me like I'd brought him a bouquet of flowers. "Of course, Lucy. Why didn't I think of that? I'll look at all of the purchases in the last fifty years. See if there's anybody who stands out."

Rafe nodded. "And what's the location of all those pieces? Anyone can use an agent to buy for them. It would be interesting to know where they are."

Once more, Theodore made a note in his little book, and as I turned away, Rafe said, "Get William to make you some warm milk."

I shook my head. "It's okay. I have some herbal teas of my own that I packed. I'll brew up one of those."

His face softened into an almost smile. "And have a magical night's sleep."

Exactly.

～

THE FOLLOWING DAY, I felt a bit stronger. Theodore and Hester came by, and we sat in Rafe's gorgeous library.

The pair had been busy. Between Theodore's good, old-fashioned legwork and Hester's computer skills, they had quite a bit of information on what had happened to the jewels designed by Jacques Cartier.

Theodore explained, "There were three Cartier brothers. Jacques is the one who moved to London. He famously became associated with British royalty and movie stars. He designed jewels for Merle Oberon and Elizabeth Taylor, as well as much of Wallis Simpson's collection." He looked at me. "Wallis Simpson, Lucy, was the wife of Edward VIII. Well, he would have been Edward VIII, but he ended up abdicating in order to marry the divorced American."

I actually did know this and the scandal that had ensued.

"Wallis liked the finer things. After she died, most of her jewelry was sold off in 1987. Much of it's never been seen again. That's the thing with these iconic jewels; they're often bought by collectors who keep a very low profile," Theodore said.

I nodded. Having had firsthand experience of how dangerous it was to display the things in public, I completely understood. "It's not like you can wear them to the grocery store or go out to the movies." I paused and felt like a vice was squeezing my ribs. "You can't even wear them to a gala event without danger and murder and theft."

"You've got to stop beating yourself up, Lucy," Hester said. It was so unlike Hester to be supportive of anyone that my jaw just about dropped. We all looked at her, and she shrugged. "It's true. Everybody makes mistakes. Lucy's was just a bit more expensive a mistake than most of them."

She had that right.

"These collectors," Rafe said, "do you have any way of finding out who they are?"

Theodore and Hester exchanged a glance. "Most auctions these days are online, of course, but even in the last few decades, it's been very common for people of note to either send an agent to do the bidding for them or bid over the phone. Elizabeth Taylor famously bought a Cartier piece over the phone while sitting by her pool in Beverly Hills," Theodore said.

It was something I could imagine Sylvia doing.

"And, speaking of Elizabeth Taylor, after her death, her jewels went on sale at auction. In 2011, the auctioneers expected to raise thirty million dollars, but the total that night was more than one hundred and fifteen million dollars," Hester added. It was obvious she was enjoying helping with the research.

"That's a lot of money," I said faintly.

"A Cartier set, not unlike Sylvia's, though made with rubies instead of emeralds, sold for five and a half million," Hester continued.

"In 2011."

"Yes."

"What do you think Sylvia's set would go for today?"

Theodore looked at me with pity. "Well north of ten million."

Oh, dear.

"Is there any chance that the set might come up for auction?" I knew it was a faint hope, but grasping at straws had become my new pastime.

Three faces looked at me with disbelief. Theodore finally said, "A reputable dealer like Christie's or Sotheby's wouldn't touch these things. It's well known that they've been stolen."

"Sylvia has catalogues from auctions going back fifty years, more probably, of Cartier pieces that she'd coveted. No doubt she'd bought some of them. Why don't you ask her for them?"

He and Rafe both turned to look at me with identical *Are you kidding me?* expressions.

"Right. Better not remind Sylvia of what she's lost. But there's a reason that Sylvia went to those auctions and not auctions for other jewelry designers. Cartier was her passion. Maybe other collectors have similar passions. I think you should find out who's been buying these things. Is there one name that keeps coming up?"

Theodore nodded. "I'll do some research."

"Was it a theft to order?" Rafe asked.

I felt like I'd found out I had a stalker. Someone who'd followed me for those jewels. The idea made me shudder. "But if that's true, they had to pull it together in a pretty short amount of time. The gala was only announced a few weeks ago, and did they even publicize that I'd be wearing the jewels?"

Hester rapidly did a Google search and then shook her

head. "The first time it's mentioned publicly is when they were stolen. I can't find any mention before the gala."

Theodore said, "That would be common practice. Only a fool would make public that such an expensive set of baubles was going to be within reach of any thief who cared to have a go."

"And there was security all over the place."

"It was a daring heist, I'll give them that," Theodore said with what almost sounded like admiration.

"So where does that leave us?" I asked, feeling more frustrated by the minute.

"It narrows down the field of plausible thieves quite a bit," Rafe said. Was he trying to make me feel better? But he didn't do that. If Rafe said something, he usually genuinely believed it to be true. He said, "It had to be someone who knew about the gala or had heard gossip about it from someone in the production company. Who knew that the jewels would be there that night?"

Theodore made a note. "People in the production company, certainly, key people in the security company..." He paused to think. "I'll find that out."

"Bryce Teddington must have known," I said.

Rafe nodded. "Then, once the thief, whoever it was, knew the stones would be there that night, they had time to put a plan in place."

He glanced at Theodore, who nodded. "But the execution was so simple, it could have been carried out in an instant."

Which left us no further ahead.

CHAPTER 15

*D*etective Inspector Ian Chisholm asked to meet me at St. Peter's College. I shouldn't have been surprised. I knew he'd be handling the homicide investigation, but somehow I had hoped that I could be kept out of it. Naturally, that wasn't possible. I thought it was strange that he wanted to meet at the college, but I didn't want him hanging around the shop scaring away the customers, so I agreed.

I wasn't working in the shop very much anyway. Between Violet and the vampires, I was pretty much at loose ends. I loved that they were all trying to protect me from Sylvia's wrath, but the shop was my purpose, my routine. Not having it left me feeling sort of adrift and with way too much time to sit around feeling both guilty and sorry for myself.

Nyx didn't help. My black cat familiar stared at me through green eyes that I felt sure were accusing. Like she was saying, *If you were a better witch, you'd have this thing figured out by now.*

I knew, now that I had free time, that I should be doing all kinds of activities I normally didn't have time for. I could cook, for instance, and fill my freezer with nutritious meals for when I was too busy. I could get a handle on my knitting. That would be an excellent use of my time, considering I ran a knitting shop. It wasn't that I wasn't improving. I was. But it did not come naturally to me.

I had another task that I should be using my free time for, and that was to become more familiar with my athame and start using the ceremonial dagger properly. I'd barely touched it since I'd brought it home.

I considered all my options, and meeting Ian at the college to walk through a murder actually seemed like a good use of my time.

I decided to walk to the college. It would take me about twenty minutes, and at least I could chalk that up as exercise. The day was cloudy and cool, so I donned a moss-green sweater over jeans and comfortable, suede walking shoes. I tied my long, blond hair back in a ponytail and set out. I loved Oxford. I especially loved walking through the oldest part, where the ancient colleges had oftentimes been built on top of even older colleges. So much had happened here. The tunnels that the vampires roamed were part of what was basically a city beneath a city. Time had a way of piling up until one civilization was buried and another just carried on over its remains. A bit like the icehouse where Bryce Teddington had been found.

I tried to shake these somber thoughts as I headed through town, dodging students and tour groups, cyclists and residents.

When I got to the college, the porter let me in. He was beginning to know my face now. He said, "The copper's waiting for you," like he needed to warn me. As though I might enter a free woman and leave in handcuffs. Which maybe I deserved.

I found DI Chisholm inspecting the open door of that secret cupboard where the ancient chamber pot still sat, while his detective peered at him from the other side of the alcove.

The director of security stood behind them as though he didn't quite know what to do. When he saw me, he looked positively relieved. "Lucy. I'm so sorry you should have to come back here again."

I felt the same way. But I tried to put him at his ease and tell him it was no bother. At the sound of my voice, Ian closed the cupboard and stood up.

He nodded his head. "Lucy. I wonder if you could walk us through the events of the other evening. Remembering everything you possibly can."

I nodded. It wasn't like I hadn't been obsessively reviewing the evening in my mind. No doubt he also had copies of the short movie and all the photographs that had been taken that evening. I went through, once again, every step I'd taken and every person I'd met. And then I told him about Bryce Teddington and his cryptic comments. "He said, where was the director, and something about the budget, and he seemed concerned about the movie stars. I wasn't quite sure what he was on about, but he kept saying there was no balance. There ought to be balance. And then he got really squirrelly and asked me to meet him in a quiet alcove. He had something important to tell me."

Ian was trying to hold on to his impassive cop face, but I knew him quite well. He was looking at me like he couldn't believe I'd done anything so stupid as to slip down a corridor to meet a virtual stranger while wearing millions of dollars' worth of jewels. Of course, in retrospect, it's always easy to see that you did a dumb thing, but at the time, Bryce Teddington had seemed sincere and nervous and just a guy trying to do the right thing.

And I suppose in that moment, I'd forgotten that I was carrying a fortune in jewels. I'd only wanted to make sure that Sylvia wasn't getting involved in something that would end badly for her. I didn't bother telling him all that. It only made me sound even more of a simpleton than I already felt.

"You agreed to meet him."

"Yes. I agreed to meet him down a quiet corridor near the ladies' room. Or at least I tried to."

He nodded. "Tell me exactly what happened."

I began to walk him through it. "There was a trolley with a huge hanging container of laundry, pulled up against the wall by the ladies' washroom. I didn't think anything of it at the time."

"But you're sure it was there?"

"I am." I remembered seeing the laundry because I'd had to step around it. Like so many things, I hadn't really noticed it at the time, but when I recollected, I had remembered it being there.

"Did you see anyone pushing it or standing beside it?"

I shook my head. I'd wracked my brains to see if I'd noticed anyone or anything out of the ordinary, but I really hadn't. "A woman came out of the ladies' room, but I think she was a waitress."

His gaze sharpened at that. "Would you recognize her again?"

"Maybe."

"If you saw a photograph?"

"I only saw her briefly. I remember the flapper outfit. I'm not sure I really noticed her face." I hadn't seen her in any of the photographs of the evening.

And then I went through again how I had showed up for my appointment with Bryce Teddington and he hadn't been there and I had been hit over the head and so on, right up until the moment that we'd found Bryce.

He'd been watching my face intently the whole time I related the ordeal. "Did you think that Bryce Teddington had stolen the jewels?"

It would be too easy to say yes. And really too easy to say no. I'd felt conflicted. I said, "I thought he was genuinely trying to do the right thing. Did I think that he was maybe a little overanxious? Yes. Did I think he was a crook who was out to steal? No."

"And when his body was discovered?"

"I suppose the easiest solution was that he'd been part of a theft ring and when he'd done his part, they got rid of him."

"You don't sound like you really believe that."

I shook my head again. "I think he was a dupe. If my instincts are right, he was a good guy. Somebody overheard us agree to meet and took the opportunity to hit me over the head and steal the jewels."

He then got me to walk him through the day that we had found Bryce and then asked the question I'd been asking myself since this happened. "Do you have any idea who might want to steal those jewels?"

I felt so frustrated I could scream. "No. It's not like a smash and grab at the local jewelry store. These things are iconic. I'm worried they'll be broken up and sold as pieces and then Sylvia—" I scrambled to reformulate that sentence and came up with, "And then Sylvia's memory would be tarnished. People won't remember her as this amazing actress but somebody whose most famous jewels were stolen. And right out from under my nose," I concluded bitterly.

He nodded. "And nobody's contacted you? Offering to sell them back? Nothing unusual has happened?"

For the third time, I shook my head. "I wish someone would contact me. I'd love to get those things back."

His face hardened. "Don't do anything stupid, Lucy. Whoever hit you over the head most likely killed Bryce Teddington. Anything suspicious happens, anything at all, and you call me."

"Of course, I will." *Of course, I wouldn't.* I'd be calling Rafe and Theodore. But once I'd called them, I'd certainly bring in the Oxford police.

"Thank you. That'll be all for now."

I made my way back through the college, and as I came out the main door, a student was going by.

But something drew my eye back to her. It was the woman who'd appeared in the background of the photographs, speaking to Bryce Teddington. Her hair was different, and she looked like a student, with a backpack on and a hoodie and jeans. But I was certain it was her. What was she doing here? Was she a student? And if so, why had she been talking to Bryce Teddington?

She glanced at me as though she felt my eyes on her and then quickly glanced away again and turned her head. Oh, the heck with it. I walked over to her. "Excuse me. I feel like I know you from somewhere."

She was clearly startled at being accosted like that. She took a step back and looked at me with a completely bland expression. "No. I don't think so." Her voice was like her, middle of the road, from somewhere in England that wasn't particularly identifiable. Her face was unremarkable. She'd pass in a crowd without causing me to look twice. And if I hadn't studied the woman in those pictures, I would have walked by her without a second glance.

I could still be wrong, but I didn't think so. "I'm sure I saw you here the other night. There was a gala."

She gave a casual laugh that seemed forced to me. "I've got one of those faces. Everyone thinks they know me. I'm just a girl-next-door type, I'm afraid." She made to move on.

I stood in front of her and blocked her path. "I don't think you're a girl next door at all. There's a police officer through that door right now. Shall we go and get him?"

My heart was beating a little too quickly. For all I knew, this woman was an international jewel thief and a murderer. But I felt quite bold being that it was the middle of the day and two Oxford CID detectives were yelling distance away.

I could almost see the way she was frantically trying to come up with something to say. "Look, I'm just a student."

"Oh yeah? What are you studying? Where's your room? Who are your professors?" She opened her mouth, and I cut her off again. "Don't even bother to lie to me. You were there that night. And you know something. What is it?"

I took a step closer, getting right up into her face. That's how freaked out I was. I was acting like a wiseguy in a mob movie. This wasn't me. Well, this was me feeling terrified about what Sylvia was going to do if I didn't get those jewels back. This woman had no idea how desperate I was. Though

I suspected she was getting some idea from the way she swiftly looked around as though seeking escape.

When it was pretty clear there wasn't any escape unless she actually was the student she was telling me she was, she dropped her tone and said, "Fine. I'm a film student. I got in by pretending to be one of the wait staff and then ditched my costume and joined the party."

"Why were you talking to Bryce Teddington?"

She looked as though she was shocked I'd seen them together, then recovered. "I have a script. I'm trying to sell it to the studio. I asked him who to talk to, and he said to make nice to Lord Pevensy."

That actually made sense, especially as there was a photo of her and his lordship snapped later, when Lord Pevensy looked peeved.

"What was written on the paper he handed to you?"

"Lord Pevensy?"

No. Peter Pan. "Bryce Teddington."

She licked her lips. "It was Annabel somebody's direct number. She's the creative director, and he said if I could get either her or Lord Pevensy to read my script, I had a chance of having my film made."

A group of students walked by, and she stepped away. "Sorry, I'm late for class."

And before I could stop her, she'd melted into the group of students.

CHAPTER 16

The vampire knitting club met that night, and I did not want to go. Gran told me she'd convinced Sylvia to attend, as though that was a comforting thought. Even the knowledge that I'd be surrounded by a dozen or so strong vampires who were my friends didn't make me comfortable to be in Sylvia's company. That vamp could carry a grudge.

"You must come, dear," Gran said, looking troubled. "We've got to move past this. I can't bear to have all this discord."

"I don't think we've passed discord when a vampire looks at you with literal bloodlust in their eyes."

She opened her mouth as though she were going to argue with me, or perhaps chide me for being too dramatic, and then shut it again without speaking. If anything, I was playing down the situation. Sylvia wouldn't even look at me, as though I were beneath not only contempt, but existence. I'd snuck a terrified glance at her face, and I would swear on my dying breath, which quite possibly would be very soon, that her eyes had gone blood-red. *Blood-red.*

I didn't want to be one of those wimpy women who relies on a man for protection, but in this case, I decided that I wasn't going to go to the club meeting that night unless Rafe was going as well. I knew I could count on him. I called him and asked his advice.

"Do I go or do I not go?"

There was a long pause. I could imagine him weighing the pros and cons. Finally, he said, "At some point you two will have to sit through a knitting circle together. I'm not certain this is the best time, but on the other hand, Sylvia may be able to help us in our investigation. I think, perhaps, you should go. I'll be on one side of you, your grandmother on the other side—"

"Gran?" I asked. I loved Gran with all my heart, but pitted against someone ruthless and violent, my sweet grandmother who'd spent her life running a knitting shop didn't seem like the best protector.

Rafe chuckled low in his throat. "The love that woman has for you is extraordinary. If I've learned anything in all my time wandering the earth, it's that love is the strongest force there is. Your grandmother would tear Sylvia to bits before she'd let her hurt you."

He didn't say the rest of the sentence, but I could hear the unspoken words. "And so would I."

And so at ten o'clock that night, with my heart doing terrified somersaults in my chest, I went down to the shop. I hadn't been working there for the last couple of days due to the aforementioned bloodlust, so it felt strange walking in. Like coming back after a holiday. I took a quick glance around the shop to make sure that everything looked to be in order. If anything, it was in better order than when I was running it. All the shelves had been tidied to within an inch of their lives.

Wools are not the easiest substances to line up perfectly. But between them, Clara and Mabel had managed it. They had shuffled around my collection of ready-to-wear sweaters, I noticed, so that their own creations were closer to the front. That made me smile. That little bit of ego. And, though they were on the homely side of beautiful, I didn't disturb the arrangement.

On the back wall, the diamond sweaters looked great. I'd have to ask the two women currently running the shop how they were selling. I had an idea that we might add some of the extra-long stockings that had been such a hit at our Christmas booth last winter.

Rafe came in the front door and looked almost angry when he saw me. "Lucy. You were to wait for me upstairs. What are you doing here in the shop all by yourself?"

"I was waiting for you." I couldn't complain that he was late, because I was about ten minutes early. "I wanted to see the shop and make sure it looked okay."

He came up very close to me. "Until Sylvia calms down, or preferably, we find her missing jewels, you are not to be alone. Do you understand me?"

In spite of the high and mighty bossing around, of course, I did understand him. I nodded. "I knew you were close. And Sylvia's not the only vampire downstairs. There's a whole lot of them that would come to my defense." I gulped. "I hope."

"Stay close to me and your grandmother tonight."

We went into the back room and, since we were the first

ones, he helped me arrange the chairs into our usual circle formation. Gran was the first one to come up from downstairs. It was so strange to see her come alone, when she did nearly everything and went nearly everywhere with her best friend, Sylvia. But Gran was drawing her line in the sand, and I really appreciated it. She was saying, by actions rather than words, that if anything went down, she was on my side.

Almost as though they'd prearranged it, which perhaps they had, Gran took the seat beside me. She pulled out her tapestry knitting bag to show me what she was working on. Gran being Gran, she'd taken that basic diamond knitting pattern and added a new twist. She'd embellished it with embroidery and bugle beads. On the green knit background, she'd embroidered Christmas baubles on a red ribbon. "I'm doing a couple of very pretty ones. I thought I'd do some children's knits, with snowmen and elves and so on, and finally, for fun, I'm doing some very ugly Christmas jumpers."

"We'll sell out," I said, picking up on her enthusiasm.

She said, "I thought it might be fun to add a couple of more elaborate sweaters to your display wall. People could buy them ready-made if they wanted to, or you could build a kit with everything already in it, including the extra directions."

I thought that was a great idea, and I told her so. The kits were not only convenient for shoppers, but there was a little extra profit in it for the hardworking proprietor of a knitting shop. She got busy with her knitting, and I pulled out my current project. You couldn't own a knitting shop for nearly two years and have tuition from some of the greatest knitters in history without learning a thing or two. I would never be passionate about knitting, but I was getting better. I'd decided that I was good enough that I could make sweaters for my mom and dad. They rarely made it back for Christmas, and I rarely made it to whatever archaeological dig site they were working on, so we mainly spent time with each other on social media and the phone. I couldn't manage a diamond sweater. It was way too complicated for my basic skills, but with a little help from friends like my grandmother, I was making my mother a lap blanket and my father a multicolored scarf. I got out my knitting and tried to get to work, but I was so nervous, my hands trembled and the needles clicked together.

Every time the trapdoor opened, I'd look up fearfully. Theodore and Dr. Christopher Weaver came up together. Hester and Carlos came next. Carlos looked disappointed to see Gran sitting beside me. He usually took that seat because we were kind of like the remedial class, and we usually sat together for companionship and mutual support. However, Hester was only too happy to have him to herself, and so the two young vampires took seats not far from me.

Clara and Mabel came in together, chattering away, and then Alfred came up looking extremely debonair in a tweed jacket and cravat. There was one seat left. Would she come?

I could not concentrate. I looked at the mass of wool on my lap and tried to remember what it was supposed to be. What I was supposed to do next.

Finally, the trapdoor opened once more. I snuck a glance up, and Sylvia rose from it like an ice queen. She stepped out and stood there for a moment as though she were about to walk on stage and make a grand entrance. And she really did. Every pair of knitting needles stopped moving. Every pair of eyes turned to her. There was absolute silence.

It might have lasted forever, except there was a meow, and suddenly Nyx came padding from the shop into the back room. It broke the moment the way a glass would shatter. And suddenly everyone was at work again, knitting and speaking in soft voices. Though every eye was keeping Sylvia in its peripheral vision, I was certain of it.

She was dressed all in black, as though she were about to attend a funeral. She had everything but the black hat with a veil hanging over her face of mourning. Theater was in Sylvia's blood, and she'd never proved it more than at that moment. If I weren't already wracked by guilt, which I was, I would have felt the cold blade of her despair pierce my heart.

Nyx looked around, and when her green-gold gaze landed on Sylvia, her back arched. She opened her mouth in a silent hiss. Then she jumped up onto my lap and, instead of curling herself in a ball to sleep, she sat there like a sentry. I'd seen statues like that in the British Museum. The cat sitting upright and guarding monuments and tombs. That's what she looked like. Not a cute kitten anymore, but a force to be reckoned with. I felt as safe as I could ever be with Rafe on one side, my grandmother on the other, and one tough, determined familiar on my lap.

Sylvia didn't say a word. She trod over to the empty chair, which put her between Carlos on one side and Alfred on the other, and sat down. She pulled out her knitting, and it was a black coat. Honestly, she was starting to look like Hester in her worst goth phase with that very pale face and garbed in nothing but black.

Our usual cheerful and industrious knitting circle seemed to have a black hole right in the middle of it, sucking all the cheer and goodwill into it. There was awkward silence and then Clara said, "Right, everybody. Let's begin our show and tell."

I thought it was cute that Clara had undertaken the emcee role. I imagined that running the knitting shop had made her feel a sense of entitlement. Whatever the reason, I was grateful to her for starting. And I could feel the strain as her voice was pitched higher than usual and she said the words much louder than necessary.

She cast around and said, "Hester, let's begin with you."

Hester brought out the diamond sweater she was working on for the shop. Gran had obviously talked her into also doing one of the pretty embellished sweaters, and she was at pains to explain how she'd decided to applique her designs onto sweaters. Instead of Christmas motifs, she'd gone for a double helix on a green background and a black music note on a white background. "I thought they'd make good gifts for college students if they were studying science or music. I've got ideas for lots of different motifs." She seemed argumentative about her idea, which meant she was worried we wouldn't like it.

But I loved her sweaters and told her so.

"Is one of them for me?" Carlos asked, laughter in his eyes.

"No!" she almost hurled the word. No one said a word about the boyfriend sweater curse, but it floated in the air. Finally, Carlos said, "Good," which nearly had Hester floating in the air.

As we went around the circle, all of our show-and-tell bits were truncated. This wasn't going to be a normal meeting, and all of us knew it. When we got to Sylvia, she offered the black cloth and said in a sepulchral tone, "I am working on my shroud."

I wanted to giggle. I really did. That kind of nervous, horrified, inappropriate giggle that you make in the middle of a solemn funeral because your nerves get the better of you. Plus, she was really laying it on thick. When was Sylvia going to need a shroud? She hadn't needed one in the last hundred years, and she looked to have a few centuries in her yet.

No one said anything, and we passed mercifully along to Alfred, who was only too happy to show off the blanket he was crocheting.

"Do you feel the cold?" Clara asked him.

He looked down his very long nose. "No. It's for charity."

We didn't even get to me, thank goodness, before Sylvia suddenly stood up and said, "Yes, yes, but I didn't come here to look at a load of badly knitted and hideously composed, amateur designs. What have you discovered about my jewels?"

To say the silence that greeted her outburst was strained was to say the least.

There was an energy in the room as though a lone human had tried to attack a pack of hungry and angry wolves. I felt the control that they were all exerting to damp down their ire.

Theodore spoke up. "Well, if it's all right with everyone, we can move on to discussing the unfortunate theft of Sylvia's Cartier set."

She made a very rude sound. "Unfortunate indeed."

I didn't even look up from my knitting because I could feel her staring directly at me for the first time since this had happened. And I didn't want to see those blood-red eyes again. It was the stuff of nightmares.

Theodore laid out what we knew so far: the discovery of Bryce Teddington's body and the mysterious woman he'd been seen talking to, who had turned up again at the school today.

"So you have nothing," she said in a furious tone.

Theodore said, "I'm still curious as to why the studio contacted you now. Why they were so anxious to get the jewels and have a gala celebration so close to the beginning of the project."

Sylvia looked thoroughly irritated at this line of questioning. "Obviously, it's a brilliant, iconic film. My performance was legendary. I'm surprised it's taken this long."

"I meant no disrespect," Theodore said hurriedly. "But your lawyer was contacted virtually out of the blue by Rune Films. Is it normal for a film to have a gala before anyone significant's been attached to the project? We know the male lead was only just out of rehab and would have jumped at the chance. There was no director, no screenwriter, no female lead. Even the costume designer had no contract. Bryce Teddington told Lucy he thought things were out of balance. Do you think he could have been right?"

"Do not speak that name to me!"

He looked at the rest of us, his cherub face a masterpiece of patience. "I wonder how we can discover why there was such a push to have the gala."

"No doubt it was a publicity stunt to encourage funding," Sylvia said.

I spoke up now. "I could call them if you'd like. I have a bit of a connection there."

Sylvia made a choking sound.

I glared at her. I was getting pretty tired of being treated this way. Enough. "I can call them and thank them for the beautiful bouquet of flowers they sent me after I was nearly killed prancing around in your jewels."

I could hardly believe I was being so brave. Both Rafe and Gran leaned in closer to me as though expecting an attack any minute. Even Nyx straightened her spine and joined me in glaring at the glamorous vampire.

The tense moment passed when she suddenly thrust her knitting back into the bag and said, "Fine. See what you can find out."

"I will. Thank you."

CHAPTER 17

*T*he next day I phoned Rune Films. I asked for Annabel, the creative director. When I gave my name, I was put through with flattering speed. "Lucy, I can't tell you how bad I feel that our beautiful evening ended in disaster. How is your poor head?"

It was nice to have someone sound so sympathetic, and I warmed to her immediately. Of course, I suspected the flowers and the gushing sympathy were their way of trying to ward off...what? A lawsuit? They'd done what they could. They'd provided security. And we hadn't even asked them to insure the jewels for that one night because they weren't insurable. At least, that's what Sylvia said. I suspected that for her, the money was immaterial. She wanted her jewels, not their monetary value.

"Why did Rune Films decide to remake this movie?"

"*The Professor's Wife?* Well, it's iconic. I studied it in film school. The timing seemed right."

"So it was your idea to remake the film?"

"Well, the truth is I've always wanted to do it, but one

needs the funding, of course. I suppose I've spoken about it often enough that when Simon Dent of Man Drake heard about it, he got hold of me. It's one of his favorite films, too, you see."

This didn't help me. "But he wasn't there for the gala."

She chuckled. "Heavens, no. Simon Dent is utterly reclusive. He's got lots of money. He's passionate about the movies. But he's a terrible germophobe. I don't think anyone's seen him in years."

"When did you last see him?"

"Never. I believe he'd dropped out of the public eye before I began my career."

"So, he's letting you take the lead. Is he only sending over money and not taking a creative stake in the production?" I didn't have a clue what I was talking about. I was only trying to keep her talking, hoping something significant would turn up.

There was a pause. "Lucy, I hate to tell you this, but I'm not sure we're going to continue with the project."

Oh, no. That was what Patricia Beeton had said too. I'd hoped, for Sylvia's sake, that that wasn't so. "I'm sorry to hear it. Is it because of the theft?"

"I honestly don't know. For our part, we were willing to continue. But this is a co-production between us at Rune Films and Man Drake. You'll have to talk to them. They're the ones pulling out. I'll get my assistant to give you their contact info."

"One more thing," I said before she could palm me off on her assistant. "Do you think Bryce Teddington had anything to do with the theft?"

I heard her say, as though she'd put her hand over the

phone, "I'll be there in a jiff." Then to me, "I honestly don't know. I'm sorry."

Then I was passed over to her assistant, Emma, who gave me the phone number for Man Drake. The call was answered immediately by Edgar Smith, and like Annabel, he was extremely sympathetic about my injuries. "I've been worried sick about you. I wanted to call, but I wasn't sure you were well enough. Or wanted to be reminded of the ghastly end to your lovely evening. How are you feeling?"

"I still have headaches," I told him. "But I'm much better now, thank you."

"It was such a terrible thing to happen. That beautiful gala, all those glamorous people, and you. I know they were made for your great-auntie, but those jewels could have been made for you. You looked stunning."

Did he think this was making me feel better? I made some fumbling answer and then said, "I'm wondering why your boss wanted to make this film."

"That's an interesting question. And the past tense, wanted, is correct. I'm afraid he's feeling this is a bad omen." He lowered his voice as though he could be overheard. "Mr. Dent is a very superstitious man. Frankly, he's afraid of everything from germs to alien invasion. Violence and theft before we'd even started shooting—it was too much for him."

Something came over me. I felt annoyed on my own behalf as well as on Sylvia's that they were shutting this film down after all we'd been through. Anger churned within me. Maybe, just maybe, if Sylvia got a remake of her film, she'd have something. Otherwise, she'd lost her precious jewels for nothing. "Please tell your boss that I need to see him. I have a few questions. I've lost a priceless collection of jewels because of him. He owes me a meeting."

I had no idea whether my brazen attempt to get myself in front of a man who hadn't seen people in years would work, but I had to try.

There was another silence. Then Edgar Smith said, "I can't promise anything. But I understand your feelings. Are you hoping to change his mind?"

"Yes."

"Right. Good for you. I'll see what I can do."

He said he'd call me back, and I hung up, astonished at my own pushiness.

Minutes later, Theodore phoned, sounding very mysterious, and asked me to meet him at Elderflower Café, which was right next door to Cardinal Woolsey's. He gave me twenty minutes' notice, which was twenty minutes for me to spend wondering why on earth a vampire would want to meet me in a tea shop.

I was right on time, even maybe a couple of minutes early, and the proprietors of Elderflower, Miss Florence Watt and Miss Mary Watt, were delighted to see me, which made me feel guilty, as I hadn't been there in a couple of weeks. I tried to visit Elderflower at least once a week for a cream tea or a sandwich or even a coffee and a chat, but I'd been busy lately with one thing and another.

The sisters were a pair of octogenarians who showed no inclination to retire anytime soon. They'd been in business as long as I'd been alive, probably longer than my parents had been alive, and no one made better scones than Mary Watt. Before I let them seat me, I glanced around and noticed that Theodore was already there.

He was sitting with a woman who had her back to me. I told them I was meeting someone and made my way over to the table.

When I caught sight of the woman's face, I had a shock. It was the woman who had been at the gala. The mysterious one who had been in intense conversation with Bryce Teddington and who'd made a pretty quick exit when I tried to tackle her on campus.

"It's you!" I said.

"Lucy," Theodore said, "I'd like to introduce Penelope Grainger."

"You have a name then," I said, somewhat sarcastically. "But is it your real one?"

"Sit down," Theodore said, and so I did. I wasn't inclined to trust this woman, and I was surprised to see Theodore looking so amiable. He leaned closer, glanced around to make sure we weren't overheard, and said, "Penelope's a private investigator. That's why she seemed vaguely familiar."

This did put a different complexion on things. I looked at her. "Really?"

She looked quite as sarcastic as I felt. "Would you like to see my license?"

Actually, I would, but I also knew that Theodore would not be easily fooled. I shook my head and instead asked her what she'd been doing at the gala that night.

Before she could speak, Florence Watt came up to take our order. Naturally, I couldn't come to Elderflower in the afternoon, even if I was trying to catch a murderer, without ordering afternoon tea. That would be a selection of sandwiches and cakes, with one fruit scone, one plain scone, Florence and Mary's homemade raspberry jam, and genuine clotted cream. They might have a menu of teas, but I always had English breakfast tea.

Penelope decided to have the same, and Theodore asked for sparkling water. When Penelope Grainger raised her eyebrows in surprise, he patted his chubby tummy and said, "I'm slimming."

She seemed to accept that, and then when Florence Watt had walked away again, she said, "I was at the gala because Bryce Teddington asked me to be."

"You mean you were his date?" I asked. They hadn't looked romantic. Also, I was pretty sure Patricia Beeton had told me they couldn't take dates.

She shook her head. "In a professional capacity."

What was this professional capacity nonsense? "You mean he hired you?"

She looked uncomfortable. "Not really."

I glanced around the room. There was a table of women who'd obviously been shopping, as bags radiated around their table. Two students were sitting side by side and going over a paper. A table of French tourists rounded out the collection of customers. I quelled my urge to shout. "Did he hire you or didn't he?"

"He asked me for a favor. No money changed hands. So officially, no, he didn't hire me."

"But you were there as an investigator."

"That's right," she confirmed.

Theodore sat back and watched, seeming quite happy for me to take the lead in the questioning. No doubt he'd already talked to her himself. Still, since I had been there and he hadn't, maybe there were things that I'd be able to think to ask that he wouldn't. Not that I could think of any right now.

Except the obvious. "Why did Bryce Teddington want you at the gala in a professional capacity?"

There was nothing subtle about my line of questioning, but then I didn't suppose there needed to be. She wasn't a suspect I was trying to worm information out of. She was a professional investigator. Allegedly. Though I still wasn't sure I trusted her. Where had she been when Bryce Teddington went missing? She hadn't investigated that very far, had she?

I glanced up to see two tiers of afternoon tea coming towards us. And once more we paused while Florence put the two cake stands in front of me and Penelope. Mary came behind her with pots of tea and cream and sugar. Theodore's bottle of sparkling water looked pretty uninteresting compared with our feast, and Florence asked him kindly if he'd like ice or lemon. He said no, he was fine, and they went off, leaving us to it.

Murder or no murder, I wasn't going to waste a minute before cutting into one of the still warm scones. I slathered it liberally with jam and cream and took the first fabulous bite. Besides, it didn't matter if my mouth was full. Penelope Grainger was the one who had a very large question to answer.

While I was chewing, I waited. Instead of digging into her sandwiches or scones, she poured tea. The brew came out pale and anemic. It wasn't ready yet, as I could have told her. It always needed a few minutes to steep.

She said, "Bryce was worried. He thought there was something funny going on, and he didn't know what it was."

I swallowed. "What did he think was going on?"

She shook her head. "Something about the budget. And the money. It didn't seem right to him."

"Could he have been embezzling?" I didn't even know where the question had come from, but somebody had killed him. It was still very possible that he was the one who had stolen the necklace. Maybe because he'd hoped to sell it and replace funds he'd stolen? Maybe simply to fatten his ill-gotten nest egg even more?

She shook her head sharply. "Bryce Teddington was the most honest person I've ever known."

CHAPTER 18

"How did you meet him?" It wasn't every day that film production accountants and private investigators rubbed shoulders.

She gave a small smile. "He was my teacher."

Theodore and I exchanged glances, both of us, no doubt, wondering what a nervous accountant had to teach this very assured, chameleon-like investigator.

She poured her tea while we pondered and then said, "I took a course in basic accounting from him. You've heard the expression 'follow the money'?"

We both nodded.

"I needed to be able to read a balance sheet quickly. To understand how to follow a trail of money. And so when Bryce Teddington taught an evening course in basic finance, I signed up. When he found out what I did for a living, he was fascinated.

"I think if he'd had it to do over again, he might have gone into forensic accounting. You see, to Bryce, a balance sheet was a beautiful thing. He loved the word balance. Everything had its place, and with equal weighting, you had this elegant structure. But have so much as one penny out of balance, and it would be like an itch he couldn't scratch until he had found the stray penny."

I nodded, suddenly recalling practically his last words to me. He'd talked about balance. And something being out of balance. So far, I could confirm that she was telling the truth. "But I don't understand what a gala evening had to do with a budget that wouldn't balance."

"I didn't understand either. He didn't want to tell me very much. He said he could be wrong. But there was a lot of money being spent on that gala, and he felt it was far too early in the process. And where he would have expected the money to be spent, it hadn't been. So I think that made it lopsided to him."

I nodded. "Unbalanced."

"That's right."

"And what did you find?"

I poured my tea. And because I'd let it steep for several minutes, it came out a rich, reddish-brown color. She said, "I tried to follow the money. In that room, the money figure was mainly Lord Pevensy. But he, like everyone else, was on his best behavior. Of course, he knew I wasn't with Rune Productions, so I pretended to be with the other company. I didn't discover much, to be honest. Except that Lord Pevensy is a man who enjoys a night out." She sighed. "I think those beautiful jewels you were wearing dazzled everyone."

I glanced up sharply. "Do you think that was the point?"

"I don't know. Possibly."

"Do you have any idea who stole them?"

She looked frustrated. "I wish I did. That wasn't my finest

night's work. After they sounded the alarm and I realized you'd been attacked and the jewels stolen, I tried to find Bryce. He was gone."

"Did you think he'd stolen the jewels?"

She hesitated. "As I said, Bryce Teddington was the most honest man I ever knew, but I'm not used to dealing with honest people. Did the thought cross my mind? Yes. I would have spent more time there and tried to find him, but obviously the police had been called. I knew they'd take everyone's name and contact information."

"And you didn't belong."

"No. And I really didn't want to be asked a lot of awkward questions. I wasn't only trying to protect myself but Bryce as well."

I supposed it made sense. Still, if she'd done a better job of investigating privately, maybe she would have found him in the laundry bin. And maybe at that point, he wasn't dead. But there was no point giving her a hard time about it. She knew that as well as I did.

"What was on the paper Bryce handed you?"

"His home address. I was to meet him there the next day."

"And did you?" I asked.

"He wasn't there." She paused. Then admitted, "I let myself in. He hadn't been home. Bed hadn't been slept in. His home was tidy, but didn't look as though he hadn't planned to come back. There was fresh milk in the fridge, apples in a bowl on the counter."

"Well?" I asked her. "You're the professional. Do you have any theories?"

She glanced at Theodore, and he nodded as though telling her it was all right to share her theory with me. No doubt they'd talked all this through before I ever got there. She said, "I do. Everyone's focusing on the missing jewels. But what if that's all just a smokescreen?"

I nearly choked on my tea. "Do you have any idea what that Cartier set is worth?"

A smile just tipped the corners of her mouth up. It was more a smirk than a smile, very superior. "Yes."

"And you think they were just collateral damage?"

"Again, yes. Think about it. If Bryce was worried enough to bring me in, then there had to be some kind of financial irregularity going on. As I said, he would not rest until his budgets balanced. Money had its own language for Bryce, and he spoke it fluently. He certainly wasn't the kind of man who could be bribed to look the other way. So my theory is that he tried to warn you that something wasn't right. He saw you there, lending your great-aunt's jewels and her image, and I think he saw you as an innocent pawn and he didn't want you to be dragged into something unsavory."

I had begun by scoffing at her theory, but the more she talked, the more I wondered if she was on the right track. "I think you might be right. He definitely wanted to tell me something that no one else would overhear."

She nodded. "Let's say someone was embezzling from the company and they knew he was getting close. They saw him go off down a deserted corridor and you follow. You were the center of attention. Well, your jewels were the center of attention. So they got rid of Bryce and then banged you over the head and took the jewels so the spotlight would stay off Bryce and stay on you."

All I could think about was Sylvia would have a fit if it turned out that someone had stolen her jewels not because they desperately wanted an original Cartier set, but to throw sand in the eyes of someone investigating an embezzlement.

"Then we have to find this person."

She nodded, and so did Theodore. At least in that, we were all in agreement.

"Okay. Where do we start?" I asked.

"Bryce's computer," Penelope said.

"Bryce's computer. What? You're going to walk in there and steal it?"

"Not me, Lucy."

I glanced up at Theodore. Like Penelope Grainger, he was staring at me the way I'd stared at the scones when they first arrived at the table. I shook my head. "Oh, no. I am not in the business of pilfering other people's computers. Especially not when they're dead."

She shook her head impatiently. "You don't need to steal the computer. I just need some files."

"Why don't you do it? You're the master of disguise. Go in and pretend you're the photocopy repair person."

"I can't get in as easily as you can, and I'm not trusted. They'd be watching me."

I turned to Theodore. "You'll have to do it."

He looked very unhappy. Computers were not Theodore's thing. "They don't know me, either. But they know you."

I said in exasperation, "What exactly is it you need?"

"I need to hack into his work files," Penelope said, leaning forward. "I want to see the budget for *The Professor's Wife* and the books for the entire company. What was it that made Bryce so uncomfortable?"

The scones were as delicious as ever, but the meeting with Penelope Grainger still left a sour taste in my mouth.

CHAPTER 19

*O*f course, when I told him, Rafe immediately vetoed the idea of me going back to Rune Films, especially when it transpired that I was supposed to steal Bryce Teddington's computer.

"Have you forgotten that Bryce Teddington ended up murdered?" he all but yelled.

Rafe so rarely raised his voice that I knew he was worried about me so I tried not to take the yelling personally. Besides, I didn't remotely want to go to Rune Films.

I explained about Penelope Grainger and her theory. He looked supremely unimpressed. "Perhaps Ms. Grainger should do her own snooping," he said coldly.

I heartily agreed, but I also needed to find the jewels. If someone at Rune Films had been embezzling, then they must need money. And even if stealing jewels worth millions was only a smokescreen, they'd still pocketed jewels worth millions. They had to have put them somewhere.

We were arguing about it when my phone rang.

Between worrying about how the shop was managing without me and, far more importantly, how I was ever going to get Sylvia's jewels back, I had to admit my witch training was right down near the bottom of my list of concerns. Unfortunately, my mentor and the head of my coven felt very differently.

Margaret Twigg was on the phone. That in itself was unusual. Her voice sounded raspy and peculiar, and I suspected telephoning people was about the last thing she ever wanted to do.

"Lucy," she said, practically shouting. "I went to the shop to see you and you weren't there. You didn't seem to be in your flat, either."

"No. How can I help you?" I wasn't going to tell her that I was staying at Rafe's place because without his protection a vampire might tear me to pieces. It was none of her business.

She said, "You're not hiding from me, are you?"

It wasn't a bad guess, but if I was hiding from anyone right now, it was Sylvia. "Of course not," I said. "I've just been busy."

"Busy studying your grimoire, I hope. And busy practicing your spells. Even better, I hope you've been spending some time with your athame."

"Yep," I replied. "All those things. It's exhausting work learning to be a great witch."

"Don't toy with me, Lucy. Untruthfulness doesn't suit you."

It was a good thing she couldn't see me, because I held the phone away and made horrible faces at it. Then I put it back to my ear. "I really have been busy." And that was the truth.

"Nevertheless, as you know, it's a full moon tomorrow night."

Oh yeah, because I spent all my spare time studying the moon cycles. I didn't say anything.

"It's the perfect night for your ceremony."

"Yeah, about that..."

"You will prepare yourself. Spend the day as much as you can alone, with your athame. You should clear your mind so you're prepared."

I really didn't like the sound of this. I bet that's what they told the teenagers back when they used to sacrifice virgins.

"Come to the stones at half past eleven."

"Why not midnight?"

She let out an irritated huff. And even on the phone, I could exactly picture her expression. The piercing blue eyes looking at me as though wondering how she ever got stuck with such an imbecile, tinged with even more irritation because she knew the imbecile had powers.

I didn't really blame her. I had a lot of sympathy for Margaret Twigg. She resented my power. I'd be perfectly happy to pass these powers on to someone else. But it didn't seem like it worked that way. I suppose we both had to work with what we had. Some of us more graciously than others.

"It will give you time to prepare and then the ceremony will take place at exactly midnight."

"All right."

"Do not be tardy. And for goddess's sake, don't forget your dagger."

~

WHEN I GOT off the phone, I discovered Hester and Carlos had stopped by. It wasn't a social call. They were excited to be part of the investigating team.

I was glad someone was.

Rafe explained what Theodore and his private eye friend wanted me to do. His tone was not enthusiastic.

After they'd heard him out, Carlos said, "But we could do this."

"Do what?" I asked. Was he planning to visit Rune Films with some story? Maybe he could pretend to be a Spanish filmmaker.

Even as I was weighing the idea, Hester jumped up and down. "Of course. Carlos and I will enter the building unseen. Security cameras don't pick us up. We'll go tonight."

"And steal Bryce Teddington's computer?" Assuming it was even still there. Maybe his replacement had it. Or, if there really was an embezzler, maybe that person had destroyed it.

She shook her head as though I was old and slow. Hester had a way of making me feel both. "We don't need to take anything away. We'll download all the files."

Carlos said, "Exactly. No one will even know we were there."

I thought this was a brilliant idea, not least because it didn't involve me trying to steal a computer from a busy office. "We'll go tonight," Carlos said.

Fine by me. I gave them a layout of the offices as I remembered them. "I don't know exactly where Bryce sat, though. Or if he even had his own office."

Hester waved my words away as though they were smoke. "We'll find it. You can count on us."

I was so relieved, I offered to drive them, but Rafe said no, Theodore could do it. "This was his idea, after all."

That organized, I was free to study my athame book and prepare for tomorrow's ordeal. Uh, ceremony.

CHAPTER 20

I don't care what anyone says, witch or no witch—it is creepy driving up to magical standing stones at eleven-thirty at night. Even though there was a full moon, the stones were located in the remains of an ancient forest, and the narrow roads that led up to the standing stones were treed on both sides, the foliage touching overhead like interlocking fingers. The silvery light that dappled through the branches and leaves didn't seem all that welcoming. Still, I'd said I'd come, and I was on my way.

Nyx sat sentry in the passenger seat of my little, red car, and a silk bag containing my athame lay on the seat beside her.

I turned to my familiar. "I don't know what we're getting into. I hope you've been through one of these, because I sure never have. And I'm counting on you, Nyx, not to let her do something dreadful to me."

Nyx stared at me with her green-gold eyes. She never spoke to me, although I had a sneaking suspicion she could have if she wanted to; she just didn't want to freak me out too much. But I would get an impression. Thoughts in my head that weren't my own. I assumed they came from her. At that moment while she stared at me, and then I turned back to look at the road before I ended up plowing into a tree, the words in my head were "Pure of heart, pure of mind, stay alert, these powers combined."

"Now you're starting to sound like Margaret Twigg," I said. But I thought I understood what Nyx was getting at. For me to fight against the inevitable was just a waste of my time and powers. Besides, if Margaret Twigg was right and she wasn't just playing some sick game with me, there was a dark tide of magic headed our way, and I was going to need every bit of my power to help keep those I loved safe.

Of course, knowing Margaret Twigg, it could all have been an elaborate charade to make me practice my magic. I wouldn't put anything past her. But, on the off chance that she was right, I'd be smart to pay attention in class.

Besides, I had spent some time with my athame today. And I'd really tried to clear my mind of clutter. In my reading, I'd learned that the athame focuses power and helps divide truth from lies. I could really use that power right now, not for any witchy business but to help get Sylvia's jewels back. I was only too glad that, because it was a ceremonial dagger, the edges were not at all sharp, because I didn't want to give Sylvia any ideas. It would be very obvious what had happened if she attacked me in the traditional way that vampires have gone after humans, but if I accidently fell on my own dagger? Who'd look at her? Well, Rafe would, obviously. But I didn't want to give her any extra tools for my destruction. Just in case.

I pulled up and noted Violet's car already in the tiny

parking lot, along with an old Morris Minor in faded green. I wondered who was invited tonight but I hadn't thought to ask.

I'd find out by getting out of the car, but I was in no hurry to do that. I checked the time, and it was only eleven twenty-seven. I had three minutes, and I was going to use every one of them. I pulled in a deep breath and let it out again. Maybe tonight would be all about magic and spells, but before I went near whatever was waiting for me, I said a spell for myself. A protection spell.

That done, I picked up the leather bag containing my dagger and opened the passenger door for Nyx. She jumped out and trotted beside me down the narrow, windy path that led to the standing stones.

I'd seen them before in moonlight, of course, because that's when most of our rituals took place. But something about them tonight struck me as particularly unearthly. The stones looked silver-tipped and magical. Where once they'd probably stood proud and all about the same size and shape, now with time, weather, and the pilfering of stone by the locals before such practices were stopped, they looked like a ring of stumpy children or dwarves.

The head stone was still standing tall and fairly straight, and as I looked at it, I had the impression that it was like the blade of my dagger. Its edges might be dull, but as it lifted its face to the moonlight, I felt its power. As I walked closer, I could feel the magic pulling me towards it. Was it me? The dagger? The combination?

I was nearly breathless with some combination of fear and excitement and just pure wonder. I was so often afraid and confused by my magic that I rarely took the time to embrace its power. I knew that it could wield damage and destruction in the wrong hands, but when channeled correctly, it was amazing.

I stepped into the ring of the stones and stood there looking around. I was all by myself. I'd have thought it was some trick except I'd seen the cars, and there were candles placed around the circle ready to be lit.

I was pretty sure they'd come from the same shop as my athame.

My sister witches were around somewhere. Maybe I was meant to do this part by myself. I walked into the center and turned in a slow circle, not because anyone had told me to but because it felt right. And then I took my athame out of its leather pouch and then out of the silk one.

Nyx came up so close to me that her soft fur brushed my ankles, and then she sat staring up at me. I raised the dagger, and moonlight glittered off it and seemed to bounce from it to the head stone. I stood that way unmoving as though I were another of the standing stones, and then from my peripheral vision, I saw three cloaked figures coming towards me from the points of the compass.

While I stood there, almost as though I'd been planted there deliberately, my cousin Violet came from the west and my great-aunt Lavinia from the east.

I turned and glimpsed the face of the man who'd sold me the athame, Alphonse Young. He stood at the southern point.

There was no gossiping, no "There you are, Lucy." They were stately and solemn as they walked closer and then paused. Finally, all our gazes turned to the head stone, and inevitably, Margaret Twigg came forward.

I was used to drama with Sylvia, but Margaret could do

drama in a different but equally powerful way. She cast the circle, and as she did so, the candles sprang to life, their flames steady and strong, unaffected by the slight breeze.

She raised her arms, lifted her face to the moon.

Violet motioned for me to hold my athame out, so I did, letting the moon touch it.

The athame began to glow with a blue light.

Margaret began to speak.

North and Earth
Stable and strong
Strengthen this dagger
Let it cut right from wrong

She turned to Great-Aunt Lavinia, who chanted to the moon in her turn:

East and Air
Pure as the breeze
Lighten this dagger
Let her use it with ease

Now Lavinia turned to the man behind me. I'd pretty much caught up with what we were doing, plus I had read the "How to Use Your Athame" book. The rhyme was simple, but I'd always found the most powerful spells to be the simplest. His voice was strong.

South and Fire
I call upon your heat
Temper this dagger

So it may mete

My cousin Violet had the final verse.

West and Water
I draw upon the spring
Cleanse this dagger
Within our sacred ring

But, of course, it was Margaret who got the last word:

Earth, Air, Fire, Water
I call on you elements four
To consecrate this dagger
Now and forevermore.
So I will, so mote it be

I didn't always enjoy spending time with Margaret Twigg, but there was no denying her power, and when the four of us got together, it was pretty impressive. I could feel the dagger vibrating in my hand, and as she ended the spell, the dagger shot blue fire like a mini-fireworks display.

Fully charged, then.

Everyone gathered around me and we all watched the dagger still glowing. The old man from the shop looked at me and his eyes looked even more strange in the moonlight. "I knew when I forged that dagger that it was for someone special."

"You made this?" I asked him.

"I did. I rarely make them anymore but I came upon the

fallen branch of an ancient yew tree and felt its power. From that I carved the handle."

That fit my hand as though he'd carved it exactly for me.

"The steel of the blade I forged from a dagger once owned by a good and powerful witch."

"It's second hand?" I was teasing, trying to lighten the heavy mood.

"It was your grandmother's," Aunt Lavinia said.

My whole body broke out in goosebumps. "No wonder the blade jumped into my hand," I said. Then I glanced from Margaret to Alphonse Young. "Wait, was that some kind of test? Putting that dagger in amongst all the others to see if I'd choose it?"

The old man shook his head. His black robes shifted like shadows. "You chose each other. I couldn't know that athame was meant for you. It could have been destined for a different witch."

"But it wasn't." I held my dagger up and it was ten times more valuable now I knew its blade had once been part of my grandmother's athame. Sylvia's Cartier jewels might fetch millions at auction, but this dagger was worth a lot more to me. However, Sylvia would not see it that way.

I looked at Margaret. "Do you think I can use this to help me find some very important missing jewels?"

Even in the moonlight, I could see the look of disdain on her face. "It's not a metal detector, Lucy. It's not like you can go around Brighton Beach and find old pennies and lager cans."

"I know that." In case she hadn't read about the theft in the local paper, I filled her in. "If the athame can bring focus and cut truth from lies, surely I can use it to help Sylvia find her missing jewelry."

Alphonse Young said, "Be very careful. Even though the blades are deliberately dulled, you don't want to be waving a dagger around. People tend to get the wrong idea."

Good point. I promised I'd keep it safely hidden if I was in public, but I could feel that my athame was going to be an important part of my witch's paraphernalia.

"Please, help me find Sylvia's jewels," I asked it as we drove back to Harrington Street. The dagger didn't so much as glow.

Nyx looked at me with pity.

CHAPTER 21

$\mathcal{I}$'d hoped that Hester and Carlos's midnight snooping would mean I no longer had to go to Man Drake and confront the elusive producer, Simon Dent, but like so many of my dreams, this turned out to be of the pipe variety.

They returned triumphant, having not only discovered Bryce Teddington's computer but having sucked all the files out of it. However, after having the files a full day, Penelope Grainger said she could find no sign of embezzlement.

"Great," I said to Theodore, who relayed the news. "What about the jewels?"

"Obviously, she didn't lead us in the right direction but, as I always say, once you close off a path, it means you're closer to the true one."

"What about the film production budget?"

He looked sad, like someone had taken his security blanket. "She discovered why Bryce Teddington had concerns about the production. The budget looked perfectly normal on the surface, but hardly any of the money had been committed. He was right to be concerned that an expensive gala was going ahead before there was a director, screenwriter, female lead or any of the key contract services engaged."

"But it doesn't make sense," I said.

"No. Perhaps Simon Dent can help unravel this tangle. Were you able to get a meeting with him?"

"Yes. Tomorrow." And, speaking of tangles, I decided I'd take my knitting along for the ride. It would give me something to do in the car on the way to and from London in the Bentley.

THE MAN DRAKE Films office could not have been more different from the Rune Films office. It barely felt like a proper office, it was so quiet, located in Grosvenor Hill in posh Mayfair, in a suite of rooms that looked comfortable, elegant, and impersonal. Edgar Smith met us at the elevator and explained the protocol. He said his boss had made an exception to agree to see us. We weren't to touch him or get too close to him, and he would like to keep the visit as brief as possible.

Since I believed this man was partly responsible for the loss of Sylvia's jewels, I thought he could have been a little more accommodating, but at least he was seeing us, and so we agreed to his terms.

Edgar led Theodore and me through a front office/reception room that contained a desk, with a computer and phone and some open files. Framed movie posters lined the walls. More memorabilia than current projects.

He knocked on a closed door and ushered us into a room where a man was sitting behind a desk. His back was to the wall, and he faced us from behind a Plexiglas shield that ran the entire way across the room. He spoke to us by way of a microphone on his desk, which amplified his voice from two speakers.

There was a comfortable seating area against the opposite wall, and here Edgar Smith motioned for us to sit.

"Can I get you anything? Tea? Coffee? Sparkling water?"

We both declined refreshment. "Very well. I'll leave you then and get back to work." And he left the room, shutting the door softly behind him. Presumably so no germs could sneak in.

Simon Dent could have been anywhere in age from about fifty-five to about seventy-five. He was overweight, with heavy jowls, wispy hair and a discontented expression on his face. His germophobe attributes were accentuated by the cloth gloves he wore. He eyed the pair of us with distaste, and even though there was a Plexiglas wall between us, he moved his chair slightly back, closer to the wall.

"Good afternoon," he said. His voice sounded weird coming from the speakers at the sides of the room.

"Good afternoon," Theodore and I echoed in unison.

He was silent then, staring at us. Well, I'd asked for this meeting, so I decided to ask the questions. I knew that Theodore was more than ready to jump in if there was something I forgot or that he needed clarification on.

"Thank you for seeing us," I began.

He inclined his head. Then, as though it were dragged out of him, he said, "I was sorry to hear about your loss."

Oh, understatement of the century.

As he had done, I indicated I'd heard him with a slight nod of my head. Still, he'd broached the subject. "That's really why we're here. As you can imagine, those jewels were virtually priceless. I'm trying to gather information. For instance, I'm wondering what made you decide to fund this remake of *The Professor's Wife?*"

He seemed to think about it for a while, as though he just threw out vast sums of money and then thought about his reasons afterward. "I've always been a cinephile. Ever since I was a lad. And that movie, *The Professor's Wife,* is one of the finest. And Sylvia Simms, incomparable."

"Incomparable indeed." So was Sylvia Strand, who had been the one who'd starred in *The Professor's Wife.* Who was Sylvia Simms? I had a fuzzy notion she was a British actress too, but she hadn't appeared in *The Professor's Wife.* Had he just made a slip of the tongue? I felt unease like a cold shiver surround me.

Theodore glanced at me, and I knew he'd caught the slip too.

Suddenly, the producer chuckled. A slow, awkward sound. "What am I saying? I meant Sylvia Strand, of course. I see too many movies. Got my Sylvias mixed up. I'm a great fan of your great-aunt. Very great fan."

I smiled and nodded as though it were an easy mistake to make. Perhaps it was. "But why this particular movie at this particular moment?" I had to ask.

He shrugged massive shoulders. "Why does one make any movie at any particular point in time? As I said, I've loved that movie since I was a boy. And now I have the means to amuse myself and with luck, millions of other people who may never have had the chance to see what a great movie it was."

Once more, Theodore and I exchanged a glance. I said, "What did you most love about the original?"

He stared at me and then suddenly looked as if he had better places to be and a lot more interesting people to talk to. "I'm not sure how this is relevant. How can I help you? As I said, I'm very sorry about your loss, but clearly it was an unfortunate coincidence."

I leaned forward in my seat. "You see, that's the thing that puzzles me. How much of a coincidence was it, really?"

"What are you suggesting, young lady? Do you think I had something to do with the loss of your great-aunt's jewels?"

I smiled sweetly. "The thought had crossed my mind."

He spread his hands as though to show there was nothing in them. With those white gloves on, it made him look like a bad mime. "I would never allow jewels in my possession that had been owned by someone else. I could never get them clean enough. Besides, I'm unmarried. Who would wear them?"

I had absolutely no idea. But I did know one thing. Something was strange about this man, and it wasn't just his alleged phobia about germs.

We asked the rest of our questions and then, feeling incredibly frustrated, I thanked the producer for his time, and Theodore and I got up, ready to leave.

When we got out to the front office, Edgar Smith was busily working at a computer. He looked up. "Any luck?" he asked. "Did you get everything you needed?"

I felt like hitting him over the head. No, I hadn't got what I needed. If anything, I now felt more confused.

We left, and I said to Theodore, "That was weird. Did it

seem to you that something was just off?"

Theodore turned to me. "You mean apart from the clown gloves and the producer speaking from within a glass box? Yes. A little."

We didn't go far, and he said, "Lucy, where does Simon Dent live?"

"How should I know?"

Theodore seemed to be off on some thought tangent of his own. "I'm going to find out."

"Okay. How?"

I wondered if he would get Hester to help him with some high-tech sleuthing, but instead his plan was incredibly simple. He was going to follow the man when he left work that evening.

"Aren't you afraid you'll miss him?"

"No. There are only two entrances and exits to this building, one at the front and one at the back. I'll keep an eye on the front, and you're to watch the other door."

I was impressed. "I'll be like your partner."

He appeared shocked. "Of course not. But you're undeniably involved in this case, and you could be helpful. I can't watch two doors at once. Let me know if you happen to see him. That's all."

I made my stealthy way to the back of the building, not that a single person in London seemed interested in what I was doing.

I found the door with no problem. All I had to do was watch it.

Five minutes passed, and I was still watching the world's most uninteresting door. No one arrived. No one left. My surveillance wasn't even enlivened by a package delivery.

I wasn't cut out for this kind of work and was bored within minutes. Plus, Theodore hadn't even given me the good side of the building to watch. I was stuck on a very uninteresting and narrow London road with little traffic and nothing to look at.

Knowing Simon Dent would recognize me, I moved to the other side of the street. I could see why most stakeouts happened in cars. At least a person could sit down and not feel like at any moment they'd be tackled by the cops for being a vagrant. It must look like I was casing places, looking to burgle them.

There were a few well-spaced young trees, some cars parked, but no foot traffic.

I decided to walk up and down a bit. At least I could get some exercise. I glanced at my watch. It was five o'clock, and it was starting to get dark.

It was a bit chilly, plus, if I was unlucky enough that Mr. Dent came out the back way, he'd recognize me, so I went into my bag. I'd brought along the scarf I was knitting my dad to pass the time. However, I decided to test-drive the project as a scarf both for warmth and disguise purposes. I tucked the end that had the knitting needle attached into my coat and did up the buttons so it couldn't escape. The finished end of the scarf went over my head. I probably looked like an old woman, but I didn't care. My hair was hidden, and my ears were warm.

Anyway, chances were Theodore would see him first.

But chance was against me. Not for the first time. The door opened as I was completing my thirty-sixth trip pacing the block, and Simon Dent emerged.

CHAPTER 22

*J*stayed on the opposite side of the street, my head ducked, peering at the producer from behind my wool scarf.

He walked down to the end of the road, never so much as glancing at me. I thought that was odd. If he was that much of a germophobe, wouldn't he have a driver? And where were his fancy, white gloves?

I texted Theodore and, not knowing what else to do, followed the man. We quickly emerged onto busier streets, and I followed the striding figure ahead of me.

We got to Oxford Street. I knew exactly where we were because Selfridges, one of my all-time favorite department stores, was across the street. To my shock, he took the stairs down to Bond Street Station. One of the busiest tube stations in London. And that's saying something.

I glanced around for Theodore but didn't see him. Muttering under my breath, I followed our quarry.

What on earth had I gotten myself into? And how did I suddenly become the assistant private investigator? Yet another job I didn't seem to be naturally suited for. Still, I did my best. I scrambled down the stairs.

Even as I was running down the stairs, I was pulling my badly knit scarf more securely over my head. Luckily, London is full of odd fashion choices, so I probably didn't even look as strange as I felt.

My biggest issue was catching sight of Simon Dent in the mayhem of London rush hour on the tube.

At first, I thought the whole thing was a waste of time and I had lost sight of the producer, but then I noticed his bulk just ahead. I had my credit card set up to let me tap my way through the turnstiles, and I followed him to the Jubilee line. He stood among the crowd of commuters on the tube station platform, and he didn't look particularly worried about the germs. There was something very odd about this guy.

He also didn't seem to take any interest in his fellow passengers, which was good for me. He got on the Tube, and I let about twenty people go on and then jumped on myself. We were at different ends of the carriage, but I kept him in my line of sight. He was reading something on his phone, completely oblivious. At Shepherds Bush, he got out, and so did I.

As soon as I was out on the street, I texted Theodore and told him where we were. His reply: Stay close but don't contact. I'm on my way.

I followed on foot as the large man headed along the street. It wasn't particularly busy, and it wasn't particularly quiet, so I thought that unless he turned around and really stared at me, he'd never notice I was tailing him. He went into a chippy, what the British call a fish-and-chip shop. Again with the germs. He came out ten minutes later with a bag that most likely contained fish and chips.

I was really curious now. I followed him a bit farther on, and he pulled out a set of keys and let himself into a dingy-looking house. Well, it was a house conversion where an old Victorian had been split into flats.

I was torn. Did I sneak in, or did I wait for Theodore?

This was my tail, and I felt quite strongly that I needed to confront "Mr. Dent."

I used the lock-opening spell I tried to use very sparingly.

Once the door was open, I didn't need any of my witchy powers to discover which flat was his. I just followed him in, and he was so oblivious that he didn't even notice that he'd been followed. He pulled out a set of keys and let himself into his flat on the ground floor.

I could have waited for Theodore. Maybe I should have waited for Theodore. But I was tired of standing around waiting. I knocked on his door. There was a peephole, and I ducked my head so that mostly he'd see the wool scarf and hopefully not recognize me. If he even answered. But while I was trying to decide whether I would magic the door open and pretend I'd found it that way if I had to, he solved my moral and ethical witch dilemma by opening the door himself.

"Yes?" He sounded irritable, like a man who is hungry and has rapidly cooling fish and chips that he'd really like to get back to.

I pulled the scarf from my head and said, "Who are you?"

He looked quite taken aback. "Who are you?" And then he looked at me closer and said, "What on earth are you doing here?"

It was such a bizarre response that I almost laughed. "I feel like I should be asking you that question. It's a pretty funny place you live in for a big, fancy producer."

He tried to pull himself up to an imposing height and look down his snooty nose at me. "I'm an eccentric. Why on earth did you follow me here?"

"Because you made a mistake. Because I don't think you are Simon Dent."

"And do you have some proof?"

It was such a lame answer, it was pathetic.

"Well, the mailbox for this flat does say Myron Schellenberg."

He let out a breath and gave it up. "I suppose you might as well come in. You've ruined my dinner now." And then he glared at me. "I'm going to keep eating. And no, you may not have a chip."

I shut the door behind me and walked into a cluttered and crowded living space. There was a tiny kitchen, a reasonably sized living room, what they called a lounge room here, and a door that stood wide open, showing a messy bedroom. The main room was furnished with a worn couch, TV, a small table and chairs.

On a coffee table in front of what was obviously his favorite seat was the fish and chips in its newspaper wrapping, the grease already seeping through. There were books and papers everywhere. Biographies of famous actors, books on method acting, and plenty of paperback copies of plays, most of them looking very well-worn. Maybe I wasn't a trained investigator like Theodore, but I wasn't an idiot.

"You're an actor."

"Guilty as charged," he said. The acrid smell of malt

vinegar assailed my nostrils as he tore open the plastic packet and liberally drizzled the stuff all over his fish and chips.

He walked over to the tiny kitchen to get himself a knife and fork and then, opening the fridge, said, "I'm having a beer. Lager? Do you want one?"

I actually did. It was tiring work being on a stakeout. So I thanked him and said I would.

There was no mention of a glass. He brought over two bottles and handed me one. I assumed since he was offering me a drink I could take a seat, and so I took a chair opposite where he was sitting.

He popped a chip in his mouth and said, "It's a tough living, but somehow I get by."

"And you were on an acting job today?"

He heaved a great sigh. "I was. And I'd very much appreciate it if you kept that fact to yourself. It's a lucrative side business, and I don't want to lose it."

"You've done it before? Impersonated Simon Dent?"

He nodded. "Probably half a dozen times."

"But why? Why would someone hire you to impersonate them?"

He shrugged his broad shoulders. "Why do rich producers do half the crazy things they do? I take my money, and I keep my mouth shut."

Right. Money. "How does he pay you?"

"Cash in an envelope. Five hundred quid, if you must know."

I sipped the cold lager, thinking. "Somebody paid you five hundred pounds to sit in an office for, what, half an hour and pretend to be someone else?"

"It's a good gig," he agreed, cutting into the crispy batter of the fish and chips.

"Who hired you?"

"The assistant fellow."

"Edgar Smith?"

He nodded. Took a sip of his beer. "That's him."

"Have you ever met Simon Dent?"

He shook his head. "I'd have liked to. Or at least see footage of him or something. It's difficult to put together a character with no clues. So I've sort of invented him."

"Wow. So you must get some kind of a script or guidance for what you're supposed to say or not say."

He nodded again. He seemed to have no problem telling me about this acting job now that I'd taken the trouble to follow him home. Which I appreciated.

"It's more guidance, really. Edgar Smith told me you'd be coming and gave me an idea of what you'd want to know and said to let you know that I had nothing to do with that theft."

He looked up. "It was a terrible thing though. I read about it in the papers. It must have been lovely having your great-aunt's expensive jewels."

I remembered his blunder in the interview. "You didn't even know who she was."

He cringed, I thought with professional embarrassment. "I'm more of a theater man than a film one. I forgot her name. Bit of a blunder."

"But then you recovered."

He dabbed a chip in a puddle of vinegar. "I had an earpiece. I was given instructions. They could hear you talking and then told me what to say in my ear."

"Who did?"

"I don't know. Voice is disguised.

"Do you think it was Simon Dent?"

"Who else would it be?"

This was getting stranger and stranger.

I got the ding of a text coming in, and I knew it was from Theodore. I ignored it. "Do you always see people at the same place?"

"Yes."

"And you've never seen Simon Dent?"

"Never set eyes on him."

"And you've never received a check? You're always paid in cash?"

"That's right." Then he looked a bit uncomfortable. "You're not going to tell anyone, are you?"

I suspected he didn't want the tax people to know about his sideline. Presumably his envelopes of cash didn't get reported to the government. I shook my head. "Not if you answer my questions."

He shrugged. "Happy to. I haven't done anything wrong."

"How did you get hired the first time?"

"I'd been in a play. Not a very good one. And I didn't have a very big part. I played some stuffy businessman. But afterwards, that assistant fellow came up to me and asked me if I'd be interested in a short-term freelance job. It paid well." He looked at me. "I can tell you, it's not very often I have someone offering me a well-paid gig. It's usually no money but good exposure. Or, 'Oh, it's for a good cause.' So I jumped at the chance of making a few bob."

"Thank you for being honest," I said.

He put the last bit of fish into his mouth and crumpled up

the now empty wrapper. "It's going to end now, isn't it? The gig."

I didn't really know how to answer that, but I suspected he might be right. All I could say was, "I'll keep your name out of it if I can."

Then he looked quite startled. "It's not illegal, is it?"

"What did you think? You were making deals, doing business impersonating someone else? You had to know you weren't on stage."

He took a deep drink of his beer. "But I just thought I was standing in for a man so reclusive he doesn't want to be seen."

"Maybe. But then why the pretense? Why not just have his business manager meet with people?"

We looked at each other, and clearly neither of us had the answer.

I thanked him for his time and left. I texted Theodore, who pulled up in the Bentley within minutes. He was pretty mad at me. After he'd finished ranting about putting myself at foolish risk and how I must never ever do anything like that again, I reminded him that he was the one who'd made me guard the back door.

I quickly realized he wasn't really that mad on his own behalf. He was more worried that Rafe was going to find out.

I quickly reassured him. I didn't want Rafe finding out I'd gone after the ersatz Simon Dent either.

As we drove back to Oxford, we talked through the whole day again. "It was extraordinary," Theodore said.

I agreed. "I think we need to look into this reclusive producer a little more deeply."

WE HASTILY CONVENED a meeting of the knitting club for that evening. I got Theodore to drop me off in front of the grocery store at the top of Harrington Street. I bought six cans of Nyx's favorite tuna and a ready meal for myself. Also fish, with potatoes and vegetables. Pretty healthy. I walked home, fed Nyx while my dinner warmed. For dessert I had two of the ginger snaps Gran still baked for me.

And while I ate, I puzzled over why a reclusive producer would hire an actor to play him. I concluded that Simon Dent was a very odd dude.

There was so much rattling around in my head that I decided to lie down, close my eyes and let the answers come to me. Nyx followed me to my bedroom and jumped on my bed, curling up in her favorite position against my side. I took my newly consecrated athame out of its bag and laid it over my heart, closed my eyes and breathed deeply. "I seek the truth," I said aloud.

I might have sought the truth, but what I got was unconsciousness. I was so tired from late nights and worry that sleep snuck up on me unawares.

I woke with a start, my heart pounding. I'd had a nightmare. It was one of those awful ones where something dark's chasing you and you run and run but know it's gaining. I'd been in an old house with a lot of rooms, that was all I could remember. I glanced at the clock. It was nine-thirty. I only had half an hour before our meeting. Nyx was also snoozing and opened one annoyed eye when I moved. I climbed over her and went to brush my teeth and hair.

Sadly, I hadn't found truth in my dream, but at least I felt more rested when I went downstairs with my knitting bag. I had no intention of knitting but I'd slipped my dagger in the bag. If there was truth and focus to be had, I was all in.

Hester was wearing the blue diamond sweater she'd been supposed to make for the back wall, looking both excited and important. She had her laptop with her.

Carlos sat beside her and the rest of us took our seats. Sylvia, by accident or design, I wasn't sure which, was in a chair a little outside the circle.

Everyone was prompt so the meeting began right at ten. Theodore was the lead investigator, and so he told the group about our meeting with Man Drake Films. He fudged around the part where I met with the actor on my own as neither of us wanted to hear Rafe's outburst.

"But why would Simon Dent hire an actor to impersonate himself?" Gran asked the question I'd been puzzling over.

Sylvia seemed less confused than the rest of us. "Producers are notoriously eccentric," she explained. "No doubt he has his reasons for remaining resolutely behind the scenes. I'm disappointed he didn't have any useful information, though." She looked at Hester and, more significantly, at Hester's computer. "And what did you find out?"

"There was no connection we could find between the people who bought deco Cartier at auction over the past fifty years and Sylvia," Hester said, looking rather crestfallen.

"None at all?" Sylvia looked really disappointed.

"No. Most of them in the recent past have been bought by a Canadian billionaire. But it looks like he started selling them off, so maybe he's not a billionaire anymore. There is real interest in Sylvia and her movies, though," Hester said, as though that might help the glum-looking vampire actress.

"There's a whole Facebook account devoted to you and your movies, you know."

Sylvia brightened at that. "There is?"

"Absolutely. Lists of where the films will be screened, places you can buy copies, lists of charity auctions where any of your mementos will be sold, stuff like that."

Sylvia immediately seemed more engaged. I had a feeling she'd be heading to her computer as soon as we were finished.

Then I realized what Hester had revealed. "Wait a minute. What do you mean about things that have been auctioned off? Sylvia's personal memorabilia?"

Hester shrugged and looked at Sylvia, who appeared offended at the question. "I may, on occasion, authorize my solicitor to provide certain items from my collection to be auctioned off in a good cause. Is there some reason why I shouldn't do whatever I wish with my own belongings?"

We all looked at her. "Sylvia, don't you think you should have told us that?" I asked.

She glared at me and then I saw the moment she realized what I was getting at. "You mean, there could be some connection?"

"Well, I think it would be worth looking at who's been buying your items. Maybe we've been going down the wrong path. Maybe it's not Cartier deco jewelry this person's after but you."

She was still devastated by the loss of her jewels, but I could see she was more flattered than horrified by this idea. "You mean I have a stalker? Fifty years after I died?"

"I think it's a possibility."

I looked at Hester, who nodded and looked very pleased

with herself. "As a matter of fact, I did some digging. If it was you and not Cartier that our thief was obsessed with, then what else might they look for?"

Hester glanced around as though someone might know the answer.

"Photographs?" Alfred suggested.

"Movie props?" Christopher Weaver added.

"Hats?" Mabel suggested. "And gloves and things?"

"Yes," Hester said. "Items associated with Sylvia Strand and with *The Professor's Wife* are extremely collectible."

I felt like I was watching a TV game show and stuck for the answer while the timer was ticking away the seconds.

"The clothes she wore on screen? Her costumes?" Alfred suggested. Oh, good one.

"Yes. What else? Big-ticket items. We're talking someone with enough dosh to buy Cartier."

"The house," I said, suddenly getting the answer right before the clanger went.

Hester nodded in my direction. "Exactly. The house where *The Professor's Wife* was partly filmed and where Sylvia used to attend parties."

"Someone bought an old manor house as a souvenir?" Sylvia asked, sounding pleased.

"I think so. I cross-referenced all the Cartier purchasers and the memorabilia purchases with the house purchaser."

"And you found a match?"

"Sort of. I found an antique dealer by the name of Ingrid Carlson who bought several Cartier pieces for an anonymous buyer. She also bought an auction lot that included Sylvia Strand photographs, and the house."

"Could this Ingrid Carlson be the real name of Simon Dent?"

"Unlikely," Hester said. "She's busy with her antique business. I doubt she has time and, unless she's hiding money that I haven't been able to find, she's not rich enough."

"I challenge anyone to hide money that you can't find," Theodore said, sounding proud of his protégé.

"Perhaps Ingrid Carlson bought the house for herself," Gran suggested. "She has to live somewhere."

"She does," Hester said, looking triumphant. "In New York."

"Could it be a second home?" Alfred asked.

"It could, but Ms. Carlson also owns a flat in Knightsbridge."

That was a fancy area of London. Would this dealer really need a New York home, a London home, and a manor house near Oxford?

Rich people often seemed to collect houses, but that was a lot of real estate. It looked like Ingrid Carlson had bought the house for someone else. Someone who was a big, big fan of Sylvia Strand.

This was the strongest lead we had. All of us knew it.

But I didn't want to jump to conclusions. "Okay, if we assume that a rich person has been buying up Sylvia's old dresses and jewels and may have bought the property where *The Professor's Wife* was filmed, it doesn't make this memorabilia-buying, crazy fan a murderer."

"I don't care whom they've murdered. Did they steal my jewels?" Sylvia asked.

"We'll have to go there to find out," Hester said.

I glanced around at the vampires. "We need a plan."

Then I realized that Rafe was glaring at Theodore, who was in turn making alarmed faces in my direction. He said, "I will make some inquiries. We mustn't startle the quarry. Hester, perhaps you and I will do a drive-by and see if there's any activity at the home."

She looked a bit surprised but readily agreed. Hester was still basking in the praise of having put together a Cartier collector and a house Sylvia was connected with.

It was an impressive achievement.

I waited until after we'd ended our meeting and the vampires had headed their separate ways, except for Rafe and Theodore. "What was that all about?" I asked Theodore. "Don't you want to make a plan?"

"Of course, I do," he said in a low voice, glancing nervously at Rafe. "But we don't want Sylvia to be involved in that plan."

There was a beat of silence, and then he said, "It could be dangerous for any mortal who got in her way."

Right. Because she'd rip them to pieces. "Okay, so what is the plan?"

"Hester and I have already checked out the place. There doesn't seem to be anyone living there. We go in tonight."

"Let me guess, in the middle of the night." I was so glad now that I'd had that pre-meeting nap.

"There's no need for you to come, Lucy," Rafe said.

"Are you kidding? I lost those jewels. I definitely plan to help find them."

Theodore looked at Rafe as though it was his decision, which irked me. Then he said, "Very well. But not a word to Sylvia."

He didn't need to worry. The less time I spent with the grudge-holding vamp, the better.

I might moan about creeping into houses that weren't mine in the middle of the night, but there were advantages. Nobody around to see what we were doing and, let's face it, vampires are sharpest at night. Me, not so much, but I could certainly get myself in the house and, maybe with the help of my athame, I could focus on clues.

As Margaret Twigg had warned me, I couldn't use it like a metal detector, unfortunately, but I felt confident that this new tool in my toolbox was going to be very useful.

CHAPTER 23

e met at two in the morning: me, Rafe, Theodore, Hester, and Carlos. Rafe had been against including two young vampires, but when I reminded him how Hester had made the breakthrough in sleuthing and how good they were with computers, he relented. Since there was no one in the house, they could check any computers that were around. There was plenty of security but, of course, the vampires didn't need to worry about being seen on film. It made them brilliant for sneaking in and out of places unseen. Me, not so much.

But Hester was pretty confident that once she got inside, she could disable the security system, and then I could waltz right in.

Accordingly, we all met at Rafe's manor house. They wore whatever they liked, but I was playing it safe, and had dressed all in black, including black leather gloves so I wouldn't leave any fingerprints behind. I was also very, very nervous.

We'd decided on two cars. Rafe and I went in the Tesla,

which is the vehicle equivalent of a dark shadow. Theodore and the young vamps went in a van that Carlos owned.

I wasn't used to sneaking around at night, and I certainly wasn't used to breaking into a place where I had no authorized reason to be. However, we didn't have enough evidence to take to the police. This was our best lead yet on finding out at least who might know something about those jewels.

The house where *The Professor's Wife* had been partly filmed was about thirty minutes' drive from Rafe's manor. It was beautiful in a grand Victorian style. I felt a small shiver of recognition from seeing its exterior as it had been in the movie. This was also the house I'd dreamed about, I was almost certain. My nightmare house. Since it was so late and only moonlight illuminated the house, it looked like the house had in the black-and-white movie.

We drove past the long, winding drive that led to the house, and parked discreetly down a narrow lane. Carlos parked his van nearby, and the five of us met up at the top of the drive.

"Are you sure it's empty?" I asked, feeling sick with nerves.

"Not positive, but nobody's been in or out since yesterday," Hester whispered.

"Wait here," Rafe said softly as we walked down the drive, all but soundlessly.

I nodded. All the windows were dark, and the place looked uninhabited.

As the four vampires continued soundlessly toward the house, I wished I had Nyx for company. I felt as frightened as though I were on the receiving end of a break-in rather than part of the break-in party.

I had a bad feeling, probably a hangover from that nightmare.

Instead of Nyx, I had my athame tucked in my bag. I'd thought it might help me focus, but now I pulled it out and held it for comfort and, if necessary, I'd brandish the dagger. It wasn't a weapon, but in the dark, it would pass as one.

About five very long minutes went by, and then Hester appeared at the open front door, beckoning. She really was good.

I went swiftly down the drive, glad the property was so large and isolated. No dogs barked, and, oddly, even as I got close to the door, no security lights came on.

I entered the house and with nothing but the faint moonlight to go by the big entrance hall looked dark and foreboding.

Hester and Carlos went off to look for computers. Theodore said we'd begin a methodical search of the downstairs, room by room. No dashing off to the likeliest spot where a safe might contain jewels. "It's important to search methodically," he whispered.

Their night vision was a hundred times better than mine so they didn't need to turn on any lights. I tried to be helpful, but I also didn't want to grope around blindly, and risk knocking things over.

Theodore began in the kitchen. He suggested I stay with him, but I told him I'd help Rafe. Rafe was searching the grand dining room and suggested I help him, but I told him I was helping Theodore. The truth was I didn't want to follow around behind either of them more encumbrance than fellow sleuth.

I might not have night vision, but I had a freshly-charged

athame and I could feel its power radiating from within my bag. While Rafe and Theodore were searching downstairs, I followed the pull of the dagger toward the stairs. Between my magic, the dagger and being in company of four vampires, I wasn't worried about being tackled by a human. I had a very strong feeling the jewels either were here or had been here. I could feel my throat, wrists and ring finger tingling.

I walked up the carpeted stairs, my steps soundless. I paused at the first landing.

Hester and Carlos were just visible in a big office. She was sitting in front of a computer tapping away while Carlos searched bookshelves.

Up one more set of stairs I climbed, and the tingling grew stronger. I was on a landing with a heavy door in front of me. I turned the handle and the unlocked door opened easily. Soundlessly.

I found myself in a large space. Someone had taken out all the walls and created a huge entertainment area that seemed to take up the entire floor of the house.

A row of theater seats upholstered in velvet, with mahogany arms, had to have come from an old cinema. A proper film projector was on a table behind the seats, and a movie was playing on a large screen that dominated the room.

It was an old black and white. *The Professor's Wife.* Without the accompanying music, this really was a silent film.

On the enormous screen, a much younger Sylvia was staring right at me. She batted those expressive eyes and spoke. The words on the screen said, "Darling. You've made me so happy." This was one of the scenes where she was wearing that Cartier set, and it hurt me to see it. I averted my gaze, and as I looked around the room, I realized it was a shrine. To Sylvia.

I didn't dare turn on any lights, so the only illumination was from the movie projector. There wasn't even moonlight as all the windows were shuttered.

It was super creepy. There were dresses on mannequins. Hats I recognized from the movie. Photographs all over the place. Every one of them was of Sylvia Strand. And, on a black, velvet mannequin, was either an extremely good copy of the Cartier set or the original.

My heart began to hammer. Please let it be the Cartier original that had been stolen.

I walked forward, my fingers itching to get at those jewels, and then I felt the pulsing power of my athame still in my hand. I glanced around swiftly, realizing I was not alone. I'd been so focused on the film and the jewels that I hadn't considered that movie might have an audience.

What had I walked into?

A voice said, cool and amused, "I had a feeling when we first met that you'd be trouble."

I turned and for the first time noticed there was someone sitting in one of the seats. He rose, and it was a slim man dressed in a dapper suit from the 1920s. It looked so much like the one Sylvia's co-star wore that I wondered if it was, in fact, the very suit. His hair was slicked back.

I still recognized him, of course.

Edgar Smith.

The supposed business manager didn't look so helpful and cheerful anymore. He looked cold. Deadly.

Murderous.

CHAPTER 24

I didn't see a weapon in his hands, but no doubt he felt confident he could take care of me.

All I needed to do was scream and the vampires would be here in a second, but I wasn't quite ready for that yet. I wanted to understand.

Help me to focus, I asked the athame silently. *Cut the truth from the lies.*

"You're not Simon Dent's business manager, are you?"

He looked at me like I was being particularly dim. "Do you think an underpaid administrator could afford all this?" He swept his arm around the space, then answered his own question. "Of course not. I inherited a fortune from my father. I was a terrible disappointment to him because he ran steel mills and I had no desire to take over that business." He rolled his eyes. "Boring."

He wandered over and gazed almost with rapture at Sylvia immortalized on the screen. "All I ever wanted was to make movies. I wanted to disappear into the world of glamour and possibilities. Being forced to learn the ropes of the steel industry sucked my soul dry. The only happiness I ever had was sitting in the dark of the cinema."

I was stunned. He couldn't be more than forty-five. "But that's not a real movie. It's a silent picture."

He turned and glared at me as though I'd insulted his baby. "You know nothing. You obviously have no taste or artistic sentiment. It was a mockery for you to inherit that wonderful woman's jewels."

"You're the one who's been buying up all of Sylvia Strand's memorabilia, aren't you?"

"Of course. I have a passion for Cartier as well, but I must admit, it began when I learned of her close friendship with the jeweler."

He glared at me. "And I'd have bought Sylvia's Cartier set happily. But you were too greedy. You wanted to keep your inheritance all to yourself. You have a tawdry mind, common-place and full of avarice."

He wasn't exactly coming across as a big-hearted philan-thropist himself.

"So you'd have bought the set except it never came on the market."

"Of course, I would. Steel money enabled me to fulfill my dream, finally, after my father...passed away."

The way he said "passed away" was so cold, I was convinced he'd had something to do with his father's demise. I'd have to get Hester to look into it. If I survived tonight.

Keep him talking, I thought. The vampires would come looking for me at some point.

"But why Sylvia? Why *The Professor's Wife?*"

"Don't you understand?" He gestured with a hand at the screen where she was laughing at the camera. "Have you ever seen anything or anyone so magnificent? If I were a magician, I would become her. But, as I can't, I do the next best thing. I sit with her every night, bringing her alive again in the only way I know how."

I wanted to snort. If he only knew. Sylvia was still around, and I doubted she'd want to cozy up to this guy.

"I buy up everything I can that belonged to her." He glared at me again. "I bought this house, as she'd filmed here and gone to parties here. I've searched for years for that diamond and emerald set. It was a major part of her, and it eluded me. I've had agents all over the world making discreet inquiries, but it never came on the market. There was no evidence it had ever been sold. So I had to lure you into the open, you and the jewels."

"Are you Simon Dent?"

He laughed. "It took you long enough to figure it out. Of course I am. I've been making movies for years. But I've never wanted anyone to know who I am. Or what my fortune is." He laughed, an eerie sound. "I'm very much a behind-the-scenes producer."

"Why did you kill Bryce Teddington?"

He seemed to think about it. "Because, Lucy, like you, he was a very nosy person. Wouldn't leave things alone. He was absolutely right, of course. The entire production was a sham. At one time I had thought about remaking *The Professor's Wife,* but how could you ever improve on perfection?"

I thought he and Sylvia might have something in common in that opinion.

"I went through all the trouble of finding a credible production company and lured you in, as I needed to find out who had the Cartier set. Extensive inquiries and a great deal of money spent on various investigators turned up the fact that it didn't seem to have ever left her family. So I had the idea that if I pretended to remake the movie, I had a pretty good chance that I might at least be able to borrow the jewels."

"With no intention of ever giving them back." I had to admit, it was a pretty good plan. Expensive and devious, but also bold and unexpected. Which was obviously why it had worked.

"You have been slow-witted but unfortunately dogged in plodding along behind me, trying to find them."

"And here I am. I'm afraid I'm going to have to take those jewels back from you." Not to mention get the cops here so he could be arrested for murder.

Again he laughed. "I offered a fabulous sum to her lawyer, through a dealer I sometimes use, to purchase the Cartier set."

What? That little nugget of information had not been passed on by Sylvia. Maybe if she'd been more forthcoming, we'd have ended up here a lot earlier. "It was obviously you who turned it down. I can't be responsible for your greed. Lucy, you're as responsible for Bryce Teddington's death as I am." He made a tutting sound. "You're a greedy, greedy girl. You don't even wear the jewels. I could tell, when you had them on at the gala, they weren't natural to you. It didn't look as though you two were even familiar with each other."

"Nevertheless, they belong to me, not you."

"Haven't you realized, my dear, that you're not leaving this house alive?"

I was about to answer in some flippant way. But I couldn't think of anything. He took a step towards me and, not knowing what else to do, I brandished my athame. Okay, the edges were deliberately blunted and I doubted it could open a letter, but at first glance, the dagger was quite imposing. Especially with the eerie glow that had changed from blue to a more purple and red hue, from the power of my emotions, presumably.

It did stop him in his tracks, and then he laughed. "Is that a prop knife? You'll have to do better than that."

I pointed the athame at him and was about to cast a spell when the door opened behind me. The hairs on the back of my neck rose. I knew without turning who it was.

"I've got this under control," I said. "Please wait outside."

Instead, there was an unearthly scream. "You terrible, little, thieving man," Sylvia shrieked. She went running towards her necklace, saying, "My jewels. My jewels. If you've so much as left a fingerprint on them…"

The man I knew as Edgar Smith made a sound like a moan. "Sylvia?" He swayed, as though he might faint.

She turned to him, magnificent. "You are a disgrace to my name and my memory," she shouted at him.

He walked towards her. Presumably he wasn't very good at math if he hadn't figured out that she had to be dead. "I did it for you. I did it all for you." He went towards her with his hands held out as though…what? They were going to embrace?

Sylvia was having none of it. She walked towards him, and I could see the deadly intent. He opened his arms as though the woman of his dreams had agreed to be his.

As her lips peeled back, I yelled, "No," but I was too late. She grabbed Edgar Smith and, well, what an angry vampire does is not pretty. That's all I'm saying.

Now it was Edgar Smith screaming. I was beside myself. "Stop it," I yelled. "Sylvia! Stop!" Luckily, the commotion drew the other vampires.

Rafe got there first. He took in the scene at a glance and raced to Sylvia, pulling her off her victim, who fell to the ground, pale and still. He held the squirming Sylvia, who was doing everything to break out of his hold.

Was it too late? I ran and dropped to my knees beside Edgar Smith. He looked deathly pale, but he was still alive. Barely. He'd lost a lot of blood though. I didn't know what to do.

Hester and Carlos came running in and went to join Rafe. I glanced up at him. He was obviously more experienced with near-death-by-vampire than I was. Hester and Carlos helped him keep Sylvia under control. Theodore arrived last. Like Rafe, he didn't waste time but simply took careful note of the situation.

"Will he make it?" I asked. My voice trembled. I didn't like Edgar Smith, or whatever his name was, and he'd murdered Bryce Teddington and stolen Sylvia's jewels, but I didn't want him to end like this.

Besides, I wasn't entirely sure how the whole vampire thing worked, but what if she'd accidently turned him into a vampire? I didn't want him in the knitting club. So I had a lot of reasons to hope Edgar Smith didn't end his life here. Now.

Theodore glanced up at me and said, "I'm not sure." Then he looked at the group still holding back Sylvia. "I suggest you escort Sylvia out of here. As soon as possible."

There was a thin dribble of blood hanging from her lip like a ruby. I saw what he meant. If they weren't holding her back, she'd finish the job she'd started.

196

Before anyone could take her anywhere, she said, her voice ice-cold, "Not without my jewelry."

He nodded once, and they escorted her to the mannequin, where she very swiftly stripped it of its jewels and, taking no chances, clasped the necklace around her throat, the earrings in her ears, the bracelets on her wrists, and the ring on her finger. The jewels looked so much better on her, like they belonged there.

Only then did she calm down and agree to leave with Hester and Carlos.

Rafe and I stayed behind with Theodore. I said, "What do we do now?"

We all looked at each other. I'd never dealt with this before, but presumably these two had. They seemed to be communicating silently, without including me. Finally, Rafe said, "It's a bit dangerous, but I don't see what choice we have."

"What are you talking about?" I asked. I hated being left out like this. Though I probably didn't want to know.

Rafe looked at me, and I could see him struggling with himself. "Lucy. I'm sorry I can't escort you home, but your flat will be safe now. Don't answer the door or the telephone to anyone but me or Theodore."

"But I could help. I don't want you two to have all the responsibility of this." Whatever this was.

He shook his head. "Trust me. It's better if you leave us now."

I glanced at Theodore, who nodded. "He's right, Lucy. We'll do this more quickly and easily without you."

I glanced around the room. The movie was still playing,

eerily. There was blood all over the floor, and who knew what Edgar would remember, assuming he survived.

As though he'd followed my train of thought, Theodore said, "Don't worry, Lucy. I'll cleanse the scene."

"But won't Edgar remember what happened to him?"

They glanced at each other again. "No."

I knew I wasn't going to get anything else out of them, so I didn't bother trying.

"All right. But I feel like a real wimp leaving you to clean up. I should help, not run home and lock myself in my flat and jump into bed and pull the covers over my head." Though, to be honest, that was exactly what I felt like doing.

"Really. You'd only be in the way," Theodore said.

So I did as I was asked. Rafe walked me to the Tesla. I glanced at him. "You trust me with your car?"

"I trust you with my life, my heart, everything I have to give."

I felt as though he'd pulled the breath right out of my lungs. He opened the door and waited while I got myself in. "I'll come and see you later and let you know how it went."

"Promise?"

"I do," and then he swiftly kissed me, and watched as I drove away.

OF COURSE, I didn't do what he told me to. I drove back to Harrington Street, but instead of going upstairs to my flat, I went downstairs into the tunnels to where Sylvia lived. I knew I was no longer in danger.

Sure enough, when I knocked, the door was opened

almost immediately by Hester. She looked more bright-eyed than ever. "Come on in," she said. "We're having a party."

Sure enough, it was a very festive atmosphere. Sylvia had cleaned herself up, and no doubt Gran had redone her makeup and hair. She was wearing a floor-length silver and black gown that looked stunning and happily wearing the set of jewels.

She looked at me for the first time with something approaching warmth since I'd lost the jewels. "Well, Lucy? What do you have to say for yourself?"

"All I can say is I am never borrowing any of your jewelry ever again."

There was general laughter, though not from Sylvia. I didn't think she'd quite forgiven me yet.

"I should have remembered the old maxim, 'Never send an understudy in and expect star power,'" she said with one eyebrow raised.

I smiled back at her, equally icily. "Or never send a mortal in to do what a vampire should do."

Gran came over and gave me a hug. "You did a wonderful job, Lucy." She kept an arm around my shoulders and turned to face Sylvia. "Don't forget it was Lucy who foiled the plot and got your jewelry back."

Sylvia sighed theatrically. But then Sylvia did everything theatrically. "Oh, very well. You are forgiven."

I had a glass of Gran's Harvey's Bristol Cream because whatever the vampires were drinking I didn't want, and we chatted over the whole extraordinary case.

I should have been exhausted, but I was so wired on adrenaline that I knew I couldn't have slept, even if I'd tried.

So I hung out with the vampire knitting club for two or three hours, and then Theodore and Rafe showed up.

Sylvia saw them first. She said, "Did you take care of him?"

Rafe looked at her satirically. "Don't you want to know if he'll live?"

"Not particularly."

"Well, I do," I said.

Theodore nodded. "He's in hospital. He needed a blood transfusion, but I'm assured he'll be fine."

"But will he remember anything?"

"No. We made sure of that."

I had no idea how they cleared people's minds or erased people's memories. It was a trick I'd like to learn.

I said, "But how did you get him to the hospital? I mean, not how did you get him to the hospital, but won't the doctors be suspicious that he's got bite marks on his neck?"

Once more, Rafe and Theodore exchanged a glance. I was getting irritated by this. "Just tell me."

"Very well. He won't have bite marks. We made it look as though he'd been attacked and someone had attempted to slit his throat but didn't complete the job."

Well, I had asked. I wanted to shriek out something like "gross," but this was their world, not mine. And they had stopped Sylvia from killing him.

"But he still has to pay for what he did to Bryce Teddington. How do we tie him to that crime?" I asked.

"Because he wrote and signed a confession."

Theodore said it so matter-of-factly that I nearly laughed. Nearly.

I didn't know whether the confession would hold up, but

all the police needed was reasonable cause to start investigating the man who'd called himself Edgar Smith, and they were going to find some very interesting stuff. Hester hadn't wasted her time in his computers. She'd found lots of shady-looking money transfers and business done under several aliases.

Edgar Smith, when he recovered, would find himself in a world of trouble.

CHAPTER 25

J was back in my shop again. And, amazingly enough, after not being here for a few days, I found I'd missed it. Clara and Mabel had done a wonderful job looking after the place, but they'd put the mohair where I liked to keep the alpaca wool and they'd lined everything up so perfectly, it was almost too neat. My personal opinion is that a knitting and wool shop should not be too pristine. You want shoppers to feel they can squeeze the balls of wool and touch things without worrying they'll get in trouble.

I was unpacking a new shipment of Teddy Lamont books and magazines. As I was putting them out on display, a blanket on the front cover of a magazine caught my eye. Mainly because it said, "An easy but stylish project." It was a blanket small enough to snuggle up with in front of the TV and hang over the back of the couch when it wasn't in use. For the first time I could remember, I actually felt the urge to knit something. Not out of obligation or so I'd have something to do during the vampire knitting club meetings, but I actually wanted to knit something. This was a huge break-through.

I was nibbling my lower lip, trying to decide whether easy meant easy enough for me or easy as in an experienced knitter would have no problem with this. But what did I have to lose?

As the shop owner, I did give myself a nice discount on wools and patterns. And I was really going to have to improve in the craft if I was going to continue running this knitting shop. I opened the magazine to the pattern and was trying to make sense of the instructions when the bells rang, announcing I had a visitor.

I looked up expecting one of my customers and dropped the magazine onto the desktop when I saw who it was.

Detective Inspector Ian Chisholm walked in, looking all business. Ever since he'd been the victim of a love potion that went wrong, I'd been slightly awkward around him. But now that I'd been involved in covering up a crime, I was a wreck.

I tried to look unconcerned and like nothing was both-ering me. Cheerfully I said, "Ian. What a surprise. Are you looking for more wool for your auntie?" His aunt was an enthusiastic knitter and one of my customers. He would often pop in to pick up things for her.

Well, not that often.

He didn't respond as cheerfully as I'd hoped. "No, Lucy. I'm here on business."

"Oh?" I could hear my voice waver a little bit on the end of the oh.

"Yes. There's been a break in the case of Bryce Tedding-ton's murder."

"Really?"

Luckily, Rafe and Theodore and I had talked about the possibility that the police would want to question me about Edgar Smith's crime and the fact that I'd been peripherally involved. Looking as innocent as I knew how, I asked, "Did you find out who did it?"

He gave me a look. I imagine it would be the kind of look a good poker player gives a really bad one who's trying to bluff. "Yes, Lucy. We did."

"That's great. Who was it?"

His gaze stayed level on me. "Care to hazard a guess?"

Great. Now he was playing games with me. "No. I wouldn't."

"It was Edgar Smith. Do you remember him?"

I knew he was toying with me, but all I could do was hang on to my innocent act. "Of course, I do. He was the business manager for the reclusive producer Simon Dent."

"It turned out he wasn't a manager. He was the producer. An extremely wealthy man. You didn't know any of this?"

I shook my head vigorously. "No. What a shock."

"It seems he was also the victim of a strange and random attack."

"Really? Edgar Smith?"

"Yes. Even more strange, he seems to have made a full confession. He even kindly wrote it down, since he's currently having trouble speaking."

I swallowed hard. "He confessed to killing Bryce Teddington? Did he say why?"

"That's the odd thing. In his written confession, he says that Bryce Teddington threatened to expose his identity. He's spent years living a double life. Pretending to be his own business manager while simultaneously living in quiet luxury."

"Sounds like a pretty weird guy."

"I'd say so. Of course, we had occasion to visit his manor house. It's not too far from here. It's where part of *The Professor's Wife* was originally filmed. Perhaps you know it?"

I could feel sweat building in my armpits. I couldn't keep this up much longer. I wasn't by nature an untruthful person, and I felt like this massive secret was expanding in my chest. If it weren't that I'd risk exposing the truth about my friends downstairs, I'd have cracked and given up everything Ian wanted to know. But I couldn't do that. I had to stay strong.

I took a deep breath. "I've heard of it, but, you know, I haven't lived in Oxford that long. I don't know the area that well."

He came closer and faced me from the other side of the cash desk. "Lucy, stop playing games with me. What do you know about those jewels?"

"You mean the jewels that were stolen from Sylvia— Sylvia Strand's estate?"

"Yes. This woman you mysteriously seem to be related to. Who bequeathed you a fortune in jewels I've never heard you mention."

"Did you find them?" I asked.

He tapped his fingers on the desktop. "Now that's a funny thing. I would have thought you'd have asked that earlier. At auction you could expect to make, what, Five million? Ten? And yet you live modestly in a flat above a knitting shop. You see, I'm a copper. And when something doesn't fit, it makes me curious."

Luckily, we'd talked this possibility through too. I'd imagined there would be some kind of a conversation around these lines, but not that it would take place in my shop or that Ian would get right in my face. I'd imagined a more polite conversation, perhaps with a superior officer, down at the station. I suspected that Ian had chosen to confront me here in my shop exactly so he wouldn't be surrounded by officialdom and I wouldn't feel like this was routine.

I shrugged, trying to look casual. "I never knew those jewels were worth so much. They were in a safety deposit box. I never wear them. Not really my style. But I couldn't get rid of them. They're family heirlooms."

"You might donate them to a museum."

I shrugged. "I might." And if they really were mine, that's exactly what I'd do.

He stared at me for another uncomfortable few seconds. "Oh, and to answer your question, we didn't find the jewels. Odd, that, isn't it? Edgar Smith claims he never had them. And yet, when we searched his manor house, there was an entire studio filled with mementos of your famous ancestor. What was she? Your grandmother?"

He knew perfectly well she hadn't been my grandmother. "My great-aunt," I said, somewhat sharply. "And it was more honorary than that there's any true bloodline."

He nodded. "Right. Funny the connections we find in families, isn't it? According to my grandfather, I'm distantly related to Robert the Bruce. Yet I cannot find any connection between anyone in your family's history and a famous movie star."

"You went poking through my family history?" I felt somewhat violated. Like he'd searched my underwear drawer.

"Just doing my job."

I'd about had enough of this uncomfortable cat and mouse game. Now I leaned forward, into his space. "Are you accusing me of a crime?"

He didn't move, but I felt his frustration. He was smart enough to know something was up, but he had no idea what. "No. That's the tricky part, isn't it? With every fiber of my being, I'm convinced you know more about this than you're telling. But why would you kill Bryce Teddington? Why would you steal your own jewels? They weren't insured. There's no insurance payout. You gain nothing by killing an accountant in a movie production company."

"Not to mention, I'd have had to hit myself over the head hard enough to knock myself out."

"And then there's that."

"I promise you, I had nothing to do with murder or a jewel theft."

"I believe you. I'm not entirely certain you didn't have something to do with its retrieval, though."

I went for mock outrage. "But you just told me you didn't find the jewels."

"No. But we did find a black velvet mannequin. Exactly the kind of thing a collector might have draped in jewels. And there was nothing on it. Nothing at all."

Trust a couple of men. I should have warned Theodore and Rafe to put something on that mannequin.

"So I guess the case stays open? You'll keep looking for the Cartier set?"

"Let's just say it won't be at the top of my priority list. And let me warn you, Lucy, if you ever wear those in public, you'll be in a world of trouble."

I shuddered. He didn't need to worry about that. I was absolutely certain those jewels would never be seen again by anyone who wasn't undead. And maybe me if Sylvia ever wanted to punish me.

Ian still didn't leave, so I said, "Is that all you wanted? To semi-threaten me?"

He let out a frustrated sigh. Dug a hand in his pocket. Pulled out a neatly folded piece of pale, blue paper and opened it. "No. I also need three balls of the Shetland Tweed in the green. And my auntie asked me to tell you how much she enjoyed your last newsletter."

Thanks for reading *Diamonds and Daggers.* I hope you'll consider leaving a review, it really helps.

Join Lucy and the vampires in her next adventure. Keep reading for a sneak peek of *Herringbones and Hexes,* the Vampire Knitting Club Book 12.

Herringbones and Hexes, Chapter 1

THE TROUBLE with working in a knitting store is that I get to see all the gorgeous patterns as they come in, the glossy magazines that lure me in with the promise that I, too, could buy a few skeins of wool, a pattern and some needles and presto, bingo, end up walking around in a designer knit sweater.

The reality is so much different. I'm trying to get better at knitting, I really am. I've figured out a few of the basics, don't drop so many stitches anymore and I've even finished a handful of garments. But I tend to fall for the more intricate designs that are, as my friends back in the states would say, way above my pay grade.

Yes, I should knit straight scarves and simple hats. Perhaps one of the simpler tea cosy patterns. But I'm an optimist at heart and while my eye is drawn to the more complex patterns, my positive thinking brain says, how hard could it be?

This particular morning, I was looking at a magazine featuring a herringbone rug. Now, I'm the first to admit that I never knew there was such a stitch as the herringbone until this magazine arrived.

I was lost in wonder when my cousin Violet looked over my shoulder. "That's pretty. It would look nice beside your bed, Lucy."

"It would." And even the thought that Vi considered me capable of making the rug made me warm to her.

"I'm sure your Gran or one of the other vampire knitters could whip that up for you in no time," she added, immediately bursting my bubble.

"No. I want to make it myself."

She flipped her long, black hair over her shoulder. "Are we running before we can walk? Or, perhaps in your case, toddling before we can walk? Crawling before we can toddle?"

Before we got to me swishing around in the womb, I held up a hand.

"Probably. But I love how knitting's all about connection.

A bit like being a witch." And, yes, I could probably use magic to ease my knitting woes, but what was the point of that? I might as well just let the vampires do all my knitting for me. I wanted to learn. No. That wasn't true. I wanted to be an accomplished knitter. Even being handy with a crochet hook would improve my confidence. Instead, I ran a knitting shop where I was daily reminded of my shortcomings.

When I'd hired my cousin Violet as my shop assistant, I'd wondered if I was doing the right thing. She was also a witch and it rankled that I'd won the struggle for our family grimoire. I'd been as surprised as she was, but witchy power's a funny thing. More innate than learned, though there was plenty of training involved, as I'd recently discovered.

I hadn't asked for it but I was learning the hard truth that me and my powers were going to be needed in some coming witchageddon that Margaret Twig, the leader of our coven, was predicting. I wasn't sure if she really foresaw dire trouble or was using it to prod me into focusing on my training, but I really was trying to master my powers.

I didn't need to strain those powers unduly to notice that Violet seemed more fidgety than usual. She kept finding things to do in the front window. She was reorganizing and dusting my winter woolens window display, which would have been both remarkable and useful on most days, since Violet wasn't usually the first to pick up the duster or the broom. However, I had just redone the window display yesterday, so there was no point to her activity. All she managed to do was annoy Nyx, who was peacefully sleeping in her usual spot, curled up in a basket of wool in my front window.

After having her nose inadvertently dusted and then

suffering the final indignity of having her basket moved while she was still in it, Nyx rose onto all fours, glared at Vi, turned all the way around to glare at me, and then jumped down and stalked to the door that separated Cardinal Woolsey's Knitting and Wool Shop from the stairway that led to my flat upstairs. She meowed insistently until I walked over and opened the door for her, whereupon she scampered upstairs, no doubt so she could enjoy the rest of her nap in peace.

I was watching Violet, wondering if I was witnessing an incipient nervous breakdown, when she jumped back and put her hand to her chest. "Maybe that's him. Is it him?"

Order your copy today! *Herringbones and Hexes* is Book 12 in the Vampire Knitting Club series.

A Note from Nancy

Dear Reader,

Thank you for reading the Vampire Knitting Club series. I am so grateful for all the enthusiasm this series has received.

I hope you'll consider leaving a review and please tell your friends who like cozy mysteries.

Review on Amazon, Goodreads or BookBub.

Your support is the wool that helps me knit up these yarns. Turn the page for a sneak peek of *The Great Witches Baking Show*.

Join my newsletter for a free prequel, *Tangles and Treasons*, the exciting tale of how the gorgeous Rafe Crosyer was turned into a vampire.

I hope to see you in my private Facebook Group. It's a lot of fun. www.facebook.com/groups/NancyWarrenKnitwits

Until next time,
Happy Reading,

Nancy

THE GREAT WITCHES BAKING SHOW

© 2020 NANCY WARREN

Excerpt from Prologue

Elspeth Peach could not have conjured a more beautiful day. Broomewode Hall glowed in the spring sunshine. The golden Cotswolds stone manor house was a Georgian masterpiece, and its symmetrical windows winked at her as though it knew her secrets and promised to keep them. Green lawns stretched their arms wide, and an ornamental lake seemed to welcome the swans floating serene and elegant on its surface.

But if she shifted her gaze just an inch to the left, the sense of peace and tranquility broke into a million pieces. Trucks and trailers had invaded the grounds, large tents were already in place, and she could see electricians and carpenters and painters at work on the twelve cooking stations. As the star judge of the wildly popular TV series *The Great British Baking Contest,* Elspeth Peach liked to cast her discerning eye over the setup to make sure that everything was perfect.

When the reality show became a hit, Elspeth Peach had been rocketed to a household name. She'd have been just as happy to be left alone in relative obscurity, writing cookbooks and devising new recipes. When she'd first agreed to judge amateur bakers, she'd imagined a tiny production watched only by serious foodies, and with a limited run. Had she known the show would become an international success, she never would have agreed to become so public a figure. Because Elspeth Peach had an important secret to keep. She was an excellent baker, but she was an even better witch.

Elspeth had made a foolish mistake. Baking made her happy, and she wanted to spread some of that joy to others. But she never envisaged how popular the series would become or how closely she'd be scrutinized by The British Witches Council, the governing body of witches in the UK. The council wielded great power, and any witch who didn't follow the rules was punished.

When she'd been unknown, she'd been able to fudge the borders of rule-following a bit. She always obeyed the main tenet of a white witch—do no harm. However, she wasn't so good at the dictates about not interfering with mortals without good reason. Now, she knew she was being watched very carefully, and she'd have to be vigilant. Still, as nervous as she was about her own position, she was more worried about her brand-new co-host.

Jonathon Pine was another famous British baker. His cookbooks rivaled hers in popularity and sales, so it shouldn't have been a surprise that he'd been chosen as her co-judge. Except that Jonathon was also a witch.

She'd argued passionately against the council's decision

to have him as her co-judge, but it was no good. She was stuck with him. And that put the only cloud in the blue sky of this lovely day.

To her surprise, she saw Jonathon approaching her. She'd imagined he'd be the type to turn up a minute before cameras began rolling. He was an attractive man of about fifty with sparkling blue eyes and thick, dark hair. However, at this moment he looked sheepish, more like a sulky boy than a baking celebrity. Her innate empathy led her to get right to the issue that was obviously bothering him, and since she was at least twenty years his senior, she said in a motherly tone, "Has somebody been a naughty witch?"

He met her gaze then. "You know I have. I'm sorry, Elspeth. The council says I have to do this show." He poked at a stone with the toe of his signature cowboy boot—one of his affectations, along with the blue shirts he always wore to bring out the color of his admittedly very pretty eyes.

"But how are you going to manage it?"

"I'm hoping you'll help me."

She shook her head at him. "Five best-selling books and a consultant to how many bakeries and restaurants? What were you thinking?"

He jutted out his bottom lip. "It started as a bit of a lark, but things got out of control. I became addicted to the fame."

"But you know we're not allowed to use our magic for personal gain."

He'd dug out the stone now with the toe of his boot, and his attention dropped to the divot he'd made in the lawn. "I know, I know. It all started innocently enough. This woman I met said no man can bake a proper scone. Well, I decided to show her that wasn't true by baking her the best scone she'd ever tasted. All right, I used a spell, since I couldn't bake a scone or anything else, for that matter. But it was a matter of principle. And then one thing led to another."

"Tell me the truth, Jonathon. Can you bake at all? Without using magic, I mean."

A worm crawled lazily across the exposed dirt, and he followed its path. She found herself watching the slow, curling brown body too, hoping. Finally, he admitted, "I can't boil water."

She could see that the council had come up with the perfect punishment for him by making the man who couldn't bake a celebrity judge. He was going to be publicly humiliated. But, unfortunately, so was she.

He groaned. "If only I'd said no to that first book deal. That's when the real trouble started."

Privately, she thought it was when he magicked a scone into being. It was too easy to become addicted to praise and far too easy to slip into inappropriate uses of magic. One bad move could snowball into catastrophe. And now look where they were.

When he raised his blue eyes to meet hers, he looked quite desperate. "The council told me I had to learn how to bake and come and do this show without using any magic at all." He sighed. "Or else."

"Or else?" Her eyes squinted as though the sun were blinding her, but really she dreaded the answer.

He lowered his voice. "Banishment."

She took a sharp breath. "As bad as that?"

He nodded. "And you're not entirely innocent either, you

know. They told me you've been handing out your magic like it's warm milk and cuddles. You've got to stop, Elspeth, or it's banishment for you, too."

She swallowed. Her heart pounded. She couldn't believe the council had sent her a message via Jonathon rather than calling her in themselves. She'd never used her magic for personal gain, as Jonathon had. She simply couldn't bear to see these poor, helpless amateur bakers blunder when she could help. They were so sweet and eager. She became attached to them all. So sometimes she turned on an oven if a baker forgot or saved the biscuits from burning, the custard from curdling. She'd thought no one had noticed.

However, she had steel in her as well as warm milk, and she spoke quite sternly to her new co-host. "Then we must make absolutely certain that nothing goes wrong this season. You will practice every recipe before the show. Learn what makes a good crumpet, loaf of bread and Victoria sponge. You will study harder than you ever have in your life, Jonathon. I will help you where I can, but I won't go down with you."

He leveled her with an equally steely gaze. "All right. And you won't interfere. If some show contestant forgets to turn their oven on, you don't make it happen by magic."

Oh dear. So they *did* know all about her little intervention in Season Two.

"And if somebody's caramelized sugar starts to burn, you do not save it."

Oh dear. And that.

"Fine. I will let them flail and fail, poor dears."

"And I'll learn enough to get by. We'll manage, Elspeth."

The word banishment floated in the air between them like the soft breeze.

"We'll have to."

Order your copy today! *The Great Witches Baking Show* is Book 1 in the series.

Ribbing and Runes - Book 13

Mosaics and Magic - Book 14

Cat's Paws and Curses - A Holiday Whodunnit

Vampire Knitting Club Boxed Set: Books 1-3

Vampire Knitting Club Boxed Set: Books 4-6

Vampire Knitting Club Boxed Set: Books 7-9

Vampire Knitting Club Boxed Set: Books 10-12

Village Flower Shop: Paranormal Cozy Mystery

Peony Dreadful - Book 1

Karma Camellia - Book 2

Highway to Hellebore - Book 3

The Great Witches Baking Show: Culinary Cozy Mystery

The Great Witches Baking Show - Book 1

Baker's Coven - Book 2

A Rolling Scone - Book 3

A Bundt Instrument - Book 4

Blood, Sweat and Tiers - Book 5

Crumbs and Misdemeanors - Book 6

A Cream of Passion - Book 7

Cakes and Pains - Book 8

Whisk and Reward - Book 9

Gingerdead House - A Holiday Whodunnit

The Great Witches Baking Show Boxed Set: Books 1-3

The Great Witches Baking Show Boxed Set: Books 4-6 (includes bonus novella)

The Great Witches Baking Show Boxed Set: Books 7-9

Vampire Book Club: Paranormal Women's Fiction Cozy Mystery

Crossing the Lines - Prequel

The Vampire Book Club - Book 1

Chapter and Curse - Book 2

A Spelling Mistake - Book 3

A Poisonous Review - Book 4

Toni Diamond Mysteries

Toni is a successful saleswoman for Lady Bianca Cosmetics in this series of humorous cozy mysteries.

Frosted Shadow - Book 1

Ultimate Concealer - Book 2

Midnight Shimmer - Book 3

A Diamond Choker For Christmas - A Holiday Whodunnit

Toni Diamond Mysteries Boxed Set: Books 1-4

The Almost Wives Club: Contemporary Romantic Comedy

An enchanted wedding dress is a matchmaker in this series of romantic comedies where five runaway brides find out who the best men really are!

The Almost Wives Club: Kate - Book 1

Secondhand Bride - Book 2

Bridesmaid for Hire - Book 3

The Wedding Flight - Book 4

If the Dress Fits - Book 5

The Almost Wives Club Boxed Set: Books 1-5

Take a Chance: Contemporary Romance

Meet the Chance family, a cobbled together family of eleven kids who are all grown up and finding their ways in life and love.

Chance Encounter - Prequel

Kiss a Girl in the Rain - Book 1

Iris in Bloom - Book 2

Blueprint for a Kiss - Book 3

Every Rose - Book 4

Love to Go - Book 5

The Sheriff's Sweet Surrender - Book 6

The Daisy Game - Book 7

Take a Chance Boxed Set: Prequel and Books 1-3

Abigail Dixon Mysteries: 1920s Cozy Historical Mystery

In 1920s Paris everything is très chic, except murder.

Death of a Flapper - Book 1

For a complete list of books, check out Nancy's website at NancyWarrenAuthor.com

Nancy Warren is the USA Today Bestselling author of more than 100 novels. She's originally from Vancouver, Canada, though she tends to wander and has lived in England, Italy and California at various times. While living in Oxford she dreamed up The Vampire Knitting Club. Favorite moments include being the answer to a crossword puzzle clue in Canada's National Post newspaper, being featured on the front page of the New York Times when her book Speed Dating launched Harlequin's NASCAR series, and being nominated three times for Romance Writers of America's RITA award. She has an MA in Creative Writing from Bath Spa University. She's an avid hiker, loves chocolate and most of all, loves to hear from readers!

The best way to stay in touch is to sign up for Nancy's newsletter at NancyWarrenAuthor.com or www.facebook.com/groups/NancyWarrenKnitwits

To learn more about Nancy and her books
NancyWarrenAuthor.com

facebook.com/AuthorNancyWarren

twitter.com/nancywarren1

instagram.com/nancywarrenauthor

amazon.com/Nancy-Warren/e/B001H6NM5Q

goodreads.com/nancywarren

bookbub.com/authors/nancy-warren

Made in the USA
Las Vegas, NV
17 October 2023

79269074R00129